TNE

UNDYING

Book Sixteen of the Hayle Coven Novels

PATTI LARSEN

ALSO BY
PATTI LARSEN

The Hayle Coven Universe

The Hunted Series
Fiona Fleming Cozy Mysteries
The Nightshade Cases
The Clone Chronicles
The Diamond City Trilogy
Didi and the Gunslinger

and much, much more.
Find your new favorite author at
pattilarsen.com
Sign up for new releases
bit.ly/pattilarsenemail

CHAPTER ONE

The sound of giggling witches filled my back yard. Giggling. And not young witches, either. The Lawrence twins twittered beside Talee Happern while Mary Gripper gossiped over her baby son, Alex, and how he was keeping her awake.

I did my best to plaster on a smile, hoping it didn't look like a grimace, wishing I was back at the gym. I'd doubled my efforts since the run-in with the Brotherhood, the twinge in my shoulder where Liander Belaisle shot me a reminder of just how serious things had become.

Deadly serious. Like almost losing Charlotte serious. The weregirl kept her distance, watching from outside the party, eyes locked on me at all times. And though she was as protective as ever—worse, sometimes, it seemed—I sensed something was wrong with her. The way she

1

flinched when I asked her a question or the way her blue eyes would fill with almost desperate anxiety.

She'd been shot herself, at the doorway to death, only the wolf inside her clinging to life, the ego of her wereside trying to hold her back. And I'd let her go, to choose life or death despite knowing I could have brought her back, maybe made things easier for her.

I tried not to feel guilty about it as I smiled wider, a glass of punch clutched in my hand as I made my way through the group of laughing women. She'd come back, by choice, my Charlotte. But she hadn't been the same since.

Near death would do that to a body, I guess.

Everyone I passed smiled at me, though no one tried to stop me, thank the elements. It freaked me out, to be honest, the way they looked at me. I tried to convince myself it wasn't awe, wonder on their faces.

A little full of ourselves these days. Gram's mental voice cackled in my head. I was about to protest when she slapped my mind with her magic. *You should be. You deserve it. As long as you don't let it screw you up when it counts.*

I glared at her over a gaggle of gray haired witches. Gram just wiggled her fingers at me in a wave and flashed her teeth.

So unhelpful.

I could have been at the gym. Working out. With Sage. Okay, so being with Sage was higher on my to-do list than working out. Though learning to fight was a close second.

I think I impressed him, too, when I came back from my brush with the Council with a new attitude.

"Kick my ass," I told him. "I need to learn how to kick yours."

Sage just nodded, smiled. And gave me the worst beating of my life. Not hard enough to leave bruises. Well, not many. But embarrassing enough I was ready to crawl in a hole and never come out.

By the time he crouched over my prone, groaning body lying on the mat, I was ready to quit.

"How was that?" Sage's smile was the same as ever, pulling against his lips, bit of scruff on his wide jaw darkening at the cleft in his chin while his sea-green eyes laughed at me.

Laughed. At. Me.

Oh *hell* no.

I punched him right in that beautiful nose of his, sending him back onto his own butt with a shocked look on his face.

Didn't last long. The smile came back ten times as bright.

"You'll do," he said.

"I'm done." I collapsed, all out of everything.

Sage stretched out next to me, waist dipping as he rolled on his side, big shoulders looming over me, cheek in his hand. "You didn't give up," he said softly. "You were down, I came in to gloat and you took your shot."

Guilt. Gulp. "Are you okay?"

He touched his nose with his glove and shrugged. "You hit like a girl." Winked.

Laughing hurt. But he was right.

A Hayle family trait. No matter how far we fell, we saved up enough strength to take the last hit.

Things progressed much better from there, though I still lost every bout. I could feel myself growing stronger, though as I side-stepped two laughing girls I felt a jab in my obliques from a blow Sage landed earlier. One of these days I'd win.

Couldn't wait.

At least getting my butt thrashed by a deliciously handsome and very sweet guy almost every day helped me to forget my boy troubles somewhat. Sage was a casual relationship, could never go beyond that and I knew it. Without magic, not even latent, all Sage and I could ever really be were friends. And I was okay with that.

Friends I could handle. Boyfriends? Yeah, not so much.

Sashenka Hensley waved from the refreshment table, dark skin glowing in the light of the setting sun. This garden party was her idea. Naturally. As my second, she took her new role very seriously, doing everything she could to bring the family closer together. They adored her completely, down to the last member. While they looked at me like I might suddenly explode all over them, they turned to Shenka as though they could tell her anything.

The stress of the Brotherhood attack on the Dumonts this past spring took a toll on all witches, but our coven was stronger and more confident than ever, mostly thanks to Shenka. I knew word got around to everyone about my part in the mess, overheard family members talking about it from time to time.

It made me uncomfortable, the way they talked about me, as bad as their awed staring. Like I was special. Unreachable. Undefeatable. I just hoped their faith in me wasn't unfounded. Even though I'd been able to muddle through so far, I had no doubt the worst was yet to come.

So weird, really, considering just a few short years ago they all accused me of being the downfall of the Hayle family. Of putting our coven at risk for no reason. And while I totally understood their previous opinions, since I'd been a bit of a brat and fought my destiny, this new hero worship they threw at me every time I came near felt worse.

I struggled with feeling alone for a long time, ever since I was young. I wasn't, not really. Would never be, not with three hitchhiking souls in my head. But the more the coven put me on their little magic pedestal, the more nervous I became.

I never wanted to let them down.

Smile. Shenka's lips widened at me, dark eyes reflecting the sunset. *You look like you're going to your own funeral.*

Oops. Guess mine slipped. I tried again only to have Shenka laugh in my head.

Okay, she sent, *no smiling. Unless someone is torturing you with magic to put that expression on your face.*

No, I sent back, a real smile rising, *but I'm being tortured, all right.*

She laughed in my head even as she laughed out loud to something one of the ladies said to her. *We're almost done*, she sent. *Thanks for being a good sport.*

Silly, I sent. *This was a great idea. Sigh. I just wish I was as good at it as you are.*

You have more important things to worry about. Shenka met my eyes. *Let me take care of the family.*

Now you know why it's so important to have a second. Gram's mind touched us both. *One you can trust. And why I pushed your ass to find one.*

Bossy. *Yeah, yeah*, I sent. I paused to steady Tara, the demon daughter of Talee who hugged me quickly after almost falling as she fled from some of the other girls in a game of tag before tearing off with peals of laughter. *You were right. You always are. Happy?*

Very. I looked up and into Gram's face. She'd approached without me noticing, standing in my space, nose almost touching mine. *Very, girl. Because I know now, no matter what, you have everything you need.*

I hugged her while she grunted before hugging me back. "Smartass grandmother," I whispered.

She kissed my cheek with a wet smack before twisting out of my grip and flouncing off with her fuzzy socked feet dancing over the grass.

Despite her happy air, why did those words feel ominous?

Chapter Two

I took a vacant seat and sipped at my water, just for something to occupy me. I felt the fine chain slide over my collarbone and I reached up to grasp the pentagram pendant Mom gave me as a gift years ago. I'd only taken to wearing it in the past few years, knowing now it held a part of her power in it. Power meant to protect me and bind me to the family. Even though she wasn't officially a Hayle witch anymore, the magic remained true to the coven.

Thinking about Mom made me sad. We hadn't talked, not really, since my release from custody. I'd tried to see her a few times, but she refused. Any attempt to reach for her with power was firmly blocked. She'd made it very clear to me she couldn't be on my side anymore. The Council magic changed her, pushed her to the brink, forcing her to do its will instead of the other way around.

Mom's deterioration was a clear indication, her premature aging and total change of personality frightening in its totality. I wished I could convince her to step down, but the thought of another witch being in her position, one not strong enough to wrangle so much magic, so much pressure, made me shake my head.

It was Mom's choice. And though I disagreed with her attitude, I understood. She couldn't save me anymore. Which meant the next time I stepped over the line, I was going to the stake.

Wow, great party ponderings, Syd.

The whole group of witches fell quiet, hushed suddenly, and I had to push up walls around me before they started to smile and chatter again. I knew my state of mind affected them through my control of the family magic, but it was hard sometimes to keep it to myself.

Right. Happy thoughts.

Which, oddly, made me think of Liam. Because there was nothing really happy between Liam and me these days. Not while his helicopter mom kept the two of us apart. I'd broken off our relationship—what little there had been thanks to Sonja O'Dane's constant need to be with Liam—before my Beltane birthday. He'd been moping and quiet ever since.

From what the black hound, Galleytrot, told me, Liam now spent most of his time in the Sidhe cavern archive, lost in books, while his mother sat with him.

Just a sad state of affairs. And while I adored Liam, loved him, I hated his mother and wished she would d—

Syd.

Bad, bad, Syd.

Another sip of water did nothing against the sudden bitterness in my mouth. Sucked. All of it. Because the guy I really wanted, the one I knew I could spend my life with, I couldn't have.

Speaking of tall, dark and scrumptious, Quaid hadn't been in touch lately either. He was my pipeline for Council and other coven information, but I hadn't heard from him in the last week or so. I took it as good news.

Had no choice.

"It's so exciting, isn't it?" I looked up, actually speechless as Penelope Anders turned and reached out to gently touch the back of my hand. Her silver hair was tinted faintly blue, brown eyes watery behind her round glasses as her lace glove scratched over my skin.

"It is?" The seat I'd taken put me beside her, but now a few of the other ladies pulled theirs around to make a little half circle with me on the end. I met their eyes, smiling, hoping it was a good smile and not the one Shenka laughed about. Rodrigua Pernicus sipped noisily from her sherry glass, wrinkled cheeks pink, small body squeezed into an antique-looking suit, a small box hat perched on her rock-hard hair.

"It certainly is." The ladies giggled. So much giggling.

I didn't know if I could stand it. "I never thought I'd live to see another coven leader come of age."

They all nodded sagely while I sat forward in my chair, ready to bolt. They were sweet, but I sucked at small talk.

"Now tell us, dear," Penelope said, voice a gasping whisper the whole yard could hear, "have you made any choices yet? Narrowed down the field, as it were?"

Okay, I clearly missed most of the conversation and now looked like an idiot. "Not sure," I said, dragging out both words as I struggled to figure out what they were talking about.

"I like that handsome Gatekeeper you've been out and about with." Rodrigua tittered over her sherry while Talee Happern leaned in and saved me.

"He's adorable." She winked at me, a flash of amber fire showing in her eyes before they reverted fully back to normal. "I wouldn't kick him out of bed for eating crackers."

The ladies laughed and slapped each other's knees while I rolled my eyes at Talee. At least my family was well adjusted enough they'd accepted the demon woman and her brood with little complaint. More than that, adopted the Happerns as though they'd always been in the coven despite the fact Talee and her two kids were demon kind and her husband a normal. Penelope snorted as she gasped for air before catching her breath. "Well, there are also lots of handsome young witches out there. Take that dashing, young Quaid."

I'd like to. Hey, wait a second. The gleam in the old lady's eye was ew worthy.

Just ew.

"Syd still has some time to decide." Rodrigua clearly wasn't one of those witches who could handle her liquor. Every witch reacted differently to alcohol. She glowed decidedly red in the nose and cheeks and swayed in her seat, though she clutched at the half-empty glass as though it kept her upright.

Decide?

I looked up as Gram joined us, meeting her faded blue eyes, her gaze sharp and careful.

Excuse me. My love life was none of their business, thanks.

"It's a big choice." Rodrigua hiccupped into one fist. "But you only have less than a year. I hope you'll let us know well before you choose so we can get to know him first."

More sage nods. Knowing stares. Expectation.

Of what?

A terrible, tight knot formed in my stomach as I realized they weren't kidding.

No, actually, they were absolutely serious.

"Of course you'll have the wedding here." Penelope clapped her white-lace gloved hands together, holding them clasped under the jowls of her chin, eyes rolled skyward. "What a gorgeous ceremony you had for Frank and that dear vampire wife of his."

Gulp.

Wedding?

What the h—

All the blood rushed from my upper body, pooling in my legs as the world went briefly dim.

"What are you talking about?" The whisper barely made it past my lips. But I knew it did, because they all looked surprised. All but Gram, who sighed and sagged, shaking her head, muttering under her breath.

"Why, everyone knows," Penelope said, happy expression fading, worry rising. I felt someone sink down beside me, a hand on my arm as the old witch went on. "You're a coven leader. Which means, by law, you must wed by your twenty-first birthday."

chapter three

I gaped. For a long, awkward, uncomfortable moment that became more awkward and uncomfortable by the heartbeat. But I simply couldn't.

Couldn't.

Comprehend—

Wedding?

Damn it, girl, Gram's mind snapped in mine. *You knew this.*

I looked up at her. *What?*

Gram hesitated, face falling. *Didn't you?*

Oh. My. Freaking. Swearword.

Shenka's voice broke the stillness, though I didn't hear a word she said. Before I knew it, she pulled me to my feet, the happy, kind tone of her voice telling me she'd smoothed things over, though the shocked looks on the watching witch's faces had to reflect my own.

Wedding?

"Syd." Shenka pulled me behind one of the large trees on the border of our property and the park, one hand tight on my arm, a smile plastered on her face, a positive mask for the outside world while her magic wrapped me in a hug. "You didn't know?"

Splutter. "What the hell?" Still trying to pull myself together over here. "What the freaking hell?"

"It's a really old law," Shenka said, voice low and soothing as my demon snarled her unhappiness and Shaylee huffed. How dare anyone tell us to do anything of the sort? Like I was supposed to know who I wanted to spend my life with at twenty-freaking-one?

"That's nice," I snarled even as my vampire tried to calm me down. Calm. Right. While my anger finally woke up and reacted to the news.

Um. Overreacted.

"Every girl knows." Shenka's power kept hugging me. "It's common knowledge."

I lashed out at Gram. *I didn't want to be a witch when I was a little girl*, I shot at her. *Did I?*

Gram's magic slammed me back. *Suck it up, buttercup*, she snarled.

Not this time. "There has to be something I can do." Anger traded off with desperation as my head swam so fast I had to clutch the tree trunk to keep from falling.

Sydlynn Thaddea Hayle. Sassafras's cold mental voice

jabbed me as my silver Persian added his two cents. I looked up at the poke, caught sight of him curled up in Tara's lap, accepting her petting even as his amber eyes flared at me. *Clearly, the discussions we had when you were a girl went right over your head. Or through the empty space between your ears. But you're a coven leader now and you have to belly up.*

Or else what? I pushed away from the tree, hands shaking, anger back with a vengeance.

Or step down, he sent. *Pick one.*

And the nasty little fur ball went back to his nasty little petting session.

"I can't." I turned from Shenka, ignoring her outstretched hand and how her magic tried to hold me, gently but firmly. "I can't just choose someone like that." Faces swirled in my mind: Liam, the demon Rameranselot whom I'd met on Demonicon, the vampire leader Sebastian. Sage.

Quaid.

Always back to Quaid.

And, superimposed over all of them, me. Maji. Immortal and likely invincible.

It took me forever to choose Liam because of the state of my being. Only to end it before it began.

I rushed to the house, not caring they stared, needing to escape their eyes, the wave of sympathy now rolling across the back yard as the rumor spread, the understanding I hadn't known.

That I didn't know I was about to be forced to sell my body for the coven.

Okay, a little harsh, but it still rang true. Yes, I'd get to choose. But what if I didn't pick someone? Would they force me? I couldn't step down, not now. I needed to keep them safe.

But marriage?

Holy crap on a hell-bound train.

Just what I needed. More complications in my life.

I'd barely reached the kitchen when the door slammed and Gram ran from the hall and into the darkening space to hug me. Her anger was gone, her sharp edges soft and kind as she pulled me against her.

"I'm sorry," she whispered. "I'm so sorry, girl."

I hugged her back, knowing she apologized for far more than this moment. Her power kept me from realizing my full potential for a long time, though I now wondered if that blockage saved me. If Gram's magic core kept me from becoming maji too early, before I could handle it.

I let her feel what I was feeling, know where my train of thought took me and felt her guilt ease.

"Things happened the way they needed to," I said, knowing now as I did how powerful destiny could be.

"If I hadn't..." Gram cleared her throat, voice thick. "I know. You're right. But I should have made sure you knew everything." She shrugged, thin shoulders rising and falling under her pink sweater.

"If you hadn't given me your magic," I said, "I'd be dead now. Or part of another coven. Or taken by the Brotherhood." The thought made me shudder. "Right?"

My alter egos all chirped their agreement, hugging Gram with their energy.

She pulled me close again, sharp nails digging into my back as she squeezed me tight.

"I'm still sorry," she said.

"Is there any way around it?" I already knew the answer, the ball of knotted stress in my gut telling me so.

Gram shook her head, white hair floating around her like a halo. "No."

And she'd know, wouldn't she? "Gram," I said. "Did you have to marry Grandfather Ivan?"

She stared at me, mute. When she spoke again, she sounded frail, almost weak.

"Your great aunt was dead," she said. "And I couldn't just abandon the family."

Tears welled, not for me. I choked on them, touched her cheek. She gripped my hand, pressing it under hers, firmly against her face.

"That's why I gave you such a hard time over that Sidhe boy," she said. "Now you understand."

She had. Told me he was too weak, that Liam wouldn't be able to stand up to me.

If only I'd known why she brought it up.

Okay then.

Married by twenty-one. In eleven months.

Choke.

CHAPTER FOUR

I left Gram in the kitchen, exiting into the driveway. I still missed seeing Mom's classic blue Mustang, her baby gone with her to Harvard. And I really needed to replace my own car Minnie, the electric blue Cooper a wreck thanks to explosives placed by the Dumont brothers.

Did I have proof they blew up my car? Technically, no.

Did I need it?

Snort.

Funny how the past flowed around me as I stood there, images of my old high-school boyfriend Brad and his big black truck, of Demetrius Strong when he was leader of the Chosen of the Light handing me pamphlets, explaining why I was evil and really had to die. Quaid on his motorcycle. I hugged myself, looked up into the gathering dark as the door eased shut behind me.

I didn't have to turn around to know who stood there, unobtrusive, watching.

"What do you think, Charlotte?" I stayed where I was, making myself breathe, trying to keep the pressure of what I'd just learned from taking me to my knees. "Should I just cut and run?"

I heard her grunt, turned at last, and caught the flare of wolf in her eyes before it retreated.

"You have a duty to your family," she growled. Literally growled, her voice vibrating with the were inside her. "If that means marrying, so be it."

Honor and duty were her thing. So her attitude didn't really surprise me. But I thought we were better friends than that.

Who was I kidding? As hard as I tried, Charlotte wasn't my friend.

"Even if it's someone I don't think is right for the job?" I took a step toward her, saw her shudder ever so slightly.

"Even so." She looked away, shoulders tight. So strange to see my bodywere show emotion physically. "For the good of the family."

I laughed, didn't mean to. Nor did I intend for the sound to be so sharp, bitter. "I've been hearing that particular phrase my whole life." And I'd given in, hadn't I? Given up, caved. Even embraced the fact this was my destiny—this and more.

But there were lines in the sand I wasn't sure I was willing to cross.

"I've given them everything," I said, without anger, as my body sagged a little, my heart sighing even as my alter egos nodded and agreed. "Can't there be something left for me?"

Charlotte's whole being snapped, the crackle of her werepower shuddering through her. "No," she said. "There can't." She spun and left me there, slamming the door behind her even as I wondered who Charlotte was really thinking of.

Because it sure as hell wasn't me.

No sulking. My vampire sent it gently, but with authority.

I know. I turned back to the dark again, the quiet of the early summer neighborhood, the sound of kids laughing in the distance, a mother calling to come inside. The distant wail of a siren silenced. The air around me stilled, the whole world soft and enveloping. Time held its breath.

Yes, I had duty to think of. Yes, I had the coven to appease and protect.

But the decision was mine.

A face crossed my mind, one I hadn't seen in a while. One I missed. Sebastian confessed his feelings to me at Uncle Frank and Sunny's wedding, though neither of us acted on them. My biggest struggle with choosing a partner came from the worry I would outlive him. But in Sebastian's case, that wouldn't be a problem.

Though children would be. I had no idea if vampires could have them.

My vampire sighed. *Unlikely*, she sent. *But knowing you, anything is possible.*

Regardless, as I stood there thinking about the delicious vampire leader, my concerns about him and Uncle Frank and Sunny grew. I'd been meaning to reach out to them again. There had been no contact in almost a year. Minding my own business held me back, knowing I was being scrutinized. But I realized I now had an excellent excuse to at least check on Sebastian.

The maji chamber under his house was the only way I knew of to contact my maji guide Iepa when she didn't initiate contact first. I'd been meaning to visit, but kept putting it off. And I wasn't about to lie to myself and make up reasons why I hadn't yet. The answer was simple.

I'd have to ask Iepa if Ameline was really necessary and I was afraid I wouldn't like the answer.

Avoidance, thy name is Syd.

No more of that. It was dark enough I knew Sebastian would be up for the night. I reached for him, let my spirit power tie in to the vampire essence and sent her out to touch him.

Nothing.

Which was totally and utterly weird. I could feel the other vampires at the mansion waking, but no Sebastian. Had he returned to Austria, to Pannera Sthol's side permanently? His Queen was a big part of his life for centuries, his decision to move his blood clan to North America a sticking point with her.

Maybe he'd given up his family and gone home to Pannera.

Hmm. Didn't sound like Sebastian. Not without saying goodbye.

Then again, how well did I really know him?

The mystery of his disappearance distracted me from my present predicament. And, though I knew going anywhere near the vampires could be seen as stepping over the line, I couldn't imagine Sebastian or any of his blood clan would raise a stink.

Charlotte. I reached for her and heard the door open immediately. "I'm going out," I said.

She didn't comment, simply came to my side as I walked down the driveway to the street, my mind touching Gram and Shenka.

Have to check something out, I sent. *Be right back.*

Got it covered, Shenka answered.

Troublemaker, Gram sent.

I hoped she was wrong.

ChAPTER FIVE

Was it a bad thing I felt relief to leave the party behind as I tore open the veil and slipped through?

Probably.

Didn't keep me from diving into a possible adventure. In fact, as I exited the veil on the front lawn of the vampire mansion, I dutifully admitted I was happiest when I had a problem to solve. Not like it was a big shocker or anything. Quaid hit the nail on the head when he said I went looking for trouble.

Well, not looking, exactly. But calm and peaceful didn't really do it for me anymore. And considering the fact every time I did fall into trouble there an excellent reason for it with a so-far-so-good outcome, I wasn't complaining.

Evasion Tactics Level: Expert.

Seriously, though, I'd been very selfish letting this whole vampire silence thing ride. I loved Uncle Frank and Sunny, missed them with a pinch of regret so sharp when I thought about it I flinched. How had I let this go for so long without checking in?

Life was complicated, but family was everything.

As I approached the front door, I told myself next stop after finding out what was up with Sebastian was a trip to Europe to see my two favorite undead. Whether Council Leader Margaret Applegate liked it or not.

We'd parted ways not too badly last time, with Margaret admitting I was in the right when the Queens tried to steal my vampire essence from me. But who knew what kind of political maneuverings went on since then? Mom was under stress from her own Council power. I could only imagine Margaret had to be, too. And from what I knew of her, she didn't have half of Mom's strength.

Enough of that for now. I'd figure out the vampire mystery, no matter what it took.

My firm knock on the door was answered in moments. Stewart, Sebastian's butler, seemed relieved to see me, though a flash of something akin to fear crossed his face a moment later.

"Coven Leader." He bowed to me.

"Hi, Stewart," I said. "Mind if we come in?"

He hesitated. Okay then. Something was definitely up

and I'd dropped the ball. When he backed away, he said, "Watch your step."

I had the distinct impression he wasn't talking about my feet.

The cool interior of the giant foyer loomed dark, only a few lights glowing in the distance down hallways running left and right, and deeper into the mansion. The gloomy feel of the place added to my unease, goosebumps rising on my arms as the door swung shut behind me.

"Just here to see Sebastian," I said as Stewart turned to face me.

"Ah," he said. "I'm afraid that won't be possible."

Alarm bells. Damn it, how had I just walked away from this and not looked into it before now?

"Mind telling me why?" The press of spirit magic touched me, some familiar, some not so much as the vampires in residence started to take notice. An undercurrent of fear ran through them, matching Stewart's.

So. Not. Good.

"I'm sorry to say," he told me in his precise tone as I spun to face him, "Sebastian DeWinter is no longer master of this blood clan."

Um, what?

"That is correct." I knew that voice. Hated it and the vampire it was attached to.

Turned slowly around. Glared with a viciousness I hadn't felt since the last time I laid eyes on Celeste.

The traitorous witch-turned-undead sycophant smiled at me, long braid swinging over her shoulder. But gone was the horse-hair quality of it, vampire magic turning it silky even as her man-hands now looked elegant and strong rather than burly. Her long, dark brown gown matched the color of her hanging braid, polished skin almost glowing in the low light.

Celeste had been an ugly witch. Vampire magic might have changed her outside to something more appealing, but she was still hideous on the inside.

"Says who?" I didn't have a leg to stand on here. Yes, I carried the vampire essence and, technically, I was actually invading another blood clan's space considering Sunny reinforced my membership in the Wilhelm family. But Sebastian was my friend. I'd gone to great lengths to rescue him from the very essence I carried and, truth be told, my fondness ran along the lines of lust as well as liking.

And I didn't abandon my friends.

Well, not forever.

Wince.

"Considering it's none of your business," Celeste said as she drifted closer, even as some of the vampires from the clan peeked in to watch, "I don't owe you an answer." Oh, but she was going to give me one, wasn't she? I could tell from the flicker of satisfaction in her eyes, the way her smile widened as she drew near. "But out of courtesy, I inform you now I've been placed in control by Her Majesty, Queen Pannera herself."

She did what? What the hell was Pannera thinking? Celeste was the enemy, or had been. Stood next to Batsheva, Pannera's opposing queen for a time, pulled her strings for the Brotherhood as far as I knew. And Pannera welcomed her into her clan?

"She's lost her mind." I didn't intend for those words to slip out, but they did. And I meant them.

Celeste merely shrugged. "Her Majesty understood I am a greater asset than enemy and offered me a place in her family." She smiled again, baring her fangs. "Explanation complete."

Not by a long freaking shot. "Where's Sebastian?" I couldn't feel him, couldn't feel much of anything. Celeste's power blocked me when I tried and, though I knew I was more than strong enough to break her wards, I couldn't risk it. Not with the Council's threat hanging over my head.

No, they weren't witches. And vampire laws were different. But I wasn't about to give Celeste the means to manipulate our laws to see me burn.

She just wasn't worth it.

But was Sebastian?

Celeste gestured at Stewart who bowed with a sad

expression and opened the door.

"Sebastian is not your concern," she said. "As leader of the Blood Clan Oberman, I'm asking you to leave."

She was kicking my ass out. Shock and frustration tumbled around on high heat in my head.

"I have to go to the maji chamber." If Celeste didn't know about it, I just let the cat out of the bag. But her evil smirk told me she'd known all along. And was probably part of the reason she was here.

I was an idiot. How could I have missed this happening right under my nose?

"You are not welcome here," Celeste hissed as she stopped within inches of my face. Charlotte snarled behind me, Celeste's eyes flashing over my shoulder to my bodywere before locking on me again. "Or your filthy dog."

I'd taken worse insults from better enemies. She'd have to try harder if she was looking to provoke me into something stupid.

A moment later I found myself standing on the top step to the entrance of the mansion, turning to see Stewart watching me with fear and grief as he closed the door behind me. Charlotte chuffed, snuffling the air, baring her teeth almost like Celeste had.

"Evil lives here now," she said.

No kidding.

So now what? Now, nothing.

Defeat sucked. With no other options, I went home, nursing my anger and concern for Sebastian. Oh, and shall we pile on worry over being cut off from the maji chamber?

Perfect.

The edge of the park was quiet, the back yard empty, party over. I paused there a moment, gathering my thoughts. Okay, so Sebastian had to be in trouble for Pannera to depose him like that. But where was he? And did this have anything to do with Uncle Frank and Sunny's silence for the last ten months?

They had to be connected, didn't they? Because that would be just my luck.

The air beside me shuddered into deeper shadow. Charlotte tried to move me aside, her strong body sliding between me and the apparition, but she'd forgotten how much working out I'd been doing. I held my ground, power pulled tight around me even as a tall, blonde vampire appeared in the cool night air.

At first I thought it was Sunny until she looked up and met my eyes. One of Sebastian's most trusted lieutenants stared back at me with a hollow, haunted expression. Anastasia looked terrible, her face paler than usual, skin sagging and wrinkled. I'd met her ages ago, back when I first encountered Sebastian and, though I hadn't liked her much, irritated by her arrogance, she'd proven to be faithful and loyal and rather friendly once I took the time to get to know her. She'd been Sebastian's third, just beneath Sunny and, I could only guess, took Sunny's place at Sebastian's side when my friend ascended to the Wilhelm throne.

Gone was the stunning vampire I knew. She shivered and hugged herself, licking her thinned lips, eyes massive in her sunken face.

"Help us," she whispered. "Please, Sydlynn. Sebastian is in trouble. And she's starving us." No need to say who "she" was. But why would Celeste starve her own blood clan? Anastasia shuddered, eyes darting from side to side before she reached for me. Charlotte growled another warning, but I ignored her, horror growing as the desperate vampire allowed me feel her weakened spirit. I gave her some strength, watched her cheeks fill out a little even as crystal tears trickled down her face. She pulled away. "The Queens have gone mad." Her lips peeled back from her white teeth, fangs bared. "I beg you," she said. "You must help. Or we're lost."

Before I could stop her, speak, act, Anastasia jerked as though she'd been struck, shuddered into shadow and vanished.

CHAPTER SIX

Gram and Shenka were in the kitchen when I stormed into the house, magic weaving around the dishes, cleaning up the mess from the party. Sassafras hissed at me as I stomped past him, barely missing his tail with my toes. He leaped onto the table to glare at me as I came to a jarring halt.

"Sebastian isn't clan leader anymore." Blurting random troubles was apparently my specialty.

Shenka seemed surprised, but Gram didn't. In fact, she looked a little guilty before her wrinkled face fell into a frown.

"Tell me you didn't keep this from me." Yeah, my anger button was on a hair trigger. Had been pushed. And pushed. And pushed—

"I knew." At least she didn't try to deny it. Even so, I vibrated with the need to shake her.

"And you thought it was a good idea to keep this little tidbit to yourself." Cold, Syd. But, well, damn it.

"There's nothing you can do," Gram said, faded blue eyes empty and flat. "And you had enough on your plate. Still do."

That kind of crap was not going to fly with two broken wings.

Gram sat with a sigh, her harsh mask fading, sadness and her own frustration showing as she reached out and stroked Sassy's fur. He instantly began to purr despite the tension in the room, his demon magic offering her comfort. "I had my own occasion to return to the vampire mansion," she said. "I found out then Sebastian wasn't in control."

Grrr. My teeth ached from grinding them together. "Do you know who is?"

She shook her head.

"Celeste Oberman." I let that particular gem sink in, watched her shoulders sag, felt instantly regretful and sank into the seat next to her. "Gram, Celeste. Of all people."

Her eyes flashed with blue fire, the family magic she still controlled rippling back toward me as her own anger woke up. "That bitch," she said.

Who undermined my mother at every turn, a Purity who couldn't bear to be a Hayle, who killed some of the finest witches I knew to protect herself. Who'd sided with

Batsheva Moromond and the Brotherhood.

Yeah. That bitch.

"She has to be up to something." I sat back, my own hand in Sassy's fur. He turned his head to stare, demon fire glowing in his gaze as his purr gained in volume. I could feel the tendrils of his comforting energy sliding up my hand, toward my heart and allowed it. "Anastasia came to me, asked for help. Said Celeste has been starving the vampires." Gram gasped softly while Shenka took the seat at the head of the table, shaking her head, eyes wide. "That the Queens have gone mad." It felt weird to repeat Anastasia's words. But I knew she was right. About Pannera, anyway, who accepted a known traitor into her blood clan.

Wait a second. Anastasia said queens.

As in—

"Sunny." I leaned forward, taking Gram's free hand in mine. "Have you talked to Uncle Frank?" Guilt slapped me all over again. Why hadn't I insisted they come for my birthday? Christmas last year? Something.

Anything.

Gram squeezed my fingers, jaw setting into a strong line. "I haven't spoken to either of them for months." She nodded once, a sharp gesture. "But you're right, girl. We've all been so wrapped up in our own messes, we've let this go on too long. Time to find out what's what."

Awesome. I stood up, her hand falling from mine.

35

"Let's go."

Gram's scowl was so deep I wasn't surprised when she kicked me firmly in the shin with one of her fuzzy socked-feet.

"'Us' nothing." She stood herself, tugging her button-up pink sweater around her thin cotton dress even as her eyes took on that faraway look telling me she spoke to someone elsewhere. I tried to eavesdrop, only to have her cut me off and glare. One sharp index finger poked me aggressively in the ribs. "You have to stay out of it."

Like hell.

I didn't get to protest. Not when someone familiar walked through the wards and knocked on the door before Varity Rhodes let herself in. The tall, thin, former Enforcer leader looked as grim as Gram, so I assumed the short message Gram managed to fire off had some of the pertinent details.

"Coven Leader." Varity bowed her head to me before hugging Gram. "Ethie."

"Feel like taking a little trip?" Gram stepped away from her friend. "My son hasn't been answering his mail."

Varity glanced sideways at me before shrugging like it was no big deal.

"I like Austria this time of year," she said. "I'll drive."

Gram grunted. "You always get us lost. I'll drive."

Seriously?

"I'm coming." I'd already made up my mind and they

weren't changing it.

Two pairs of eyes stared me down, two old ladies, their mutual power snapping and crackling, sending me back a step.

"You're staying put." Varity pointed at me then at the floor under my feet. "Don't think I'm out of the loop, young lady. The Council is watching you like you're something good for dinner, just waiting for you to screw up. And while the vampires aren't in our purview, there's no way any granddaughter of Ethie's is going to the stake on my watch because some anxious-ass Council member decided you stepped over a line."

Bossy pants.

"Let me handle this." Gram turned from me, offered her hand to her old friend. "We'll be back before you know it."

A million protests broke over my mind.

Didn't matter.

Damn them.

I watched them leave, tension poking me in the back, the need to act, to help, to do something driving me to shake where I stood.

But they were right.

How was I supposed to get anything done if I had to look over my shoulder every two seconds?

Shenka rose and came to my side, hand on my shoulder, turning me gently around. The empathy in her eyes told me she understood.

And was almost more than I could stand.

"They might as well have left me in that pretty prison at Harvard," I said, turning from Shenka. Meeting Sassy's eyes. "I'm still in a cell."

Sassafras sighed. "I hate to agree with you," he said. "But you're correct. For now, all you can do is allow others to handle things. There will come a time when breaking the Council's shackles will be worth the risk. But not this time."

I didn't get a chance to reply.

Syd! Liam's mental voice lurched against mine as I felt him surge free of the wards around the Gate cavern and into the open air. His touch was so strong I saw him standing in the dark basement of town hall, eyes wide, whole body shaking.

Liam. I reached back, hugging him with my magic, surprised peripherally to find his clinging mother wasn't hovering in the background. *What's going on?*

The Sidhe. He let me feel his fear. *Something is wrong.*

—*Decay. Crumbling death. Loss. Crushing me, pulling at my breath, my strength, the very earth beneath me weak and failing as Shaylee cried out in pain*—

No way was I holding back. Sassafras's right time to act had just shown up.

chapter seven

Charlotte stayed close behind me as I bolted out of the kitchen, part way into the street before I tore a hole in the veil and leaped through. I had just enough presence of mind to shield the sight from the normals on my block, barely inside the rubber membrane long enough to feel the touch of my demon grandmother's soul hovering around me before I hurtled out of the other end and into the side door of town hall.

Liam met me at the basement stairs, arms engulfing me as I panted to a halt. His deep, earthy scent mixed with fabric softener and the warmth of him helped to slow my heart a little, but his own panic came through loud and clear.

"Come on." He turned and bounded down the stairs, me on his heels, passing through the wards. It wasn't until I grabbed Charlotte's hand and guided her through the

Sidhe protections I realized Liam wasn't alone.

But it wasn't the giant black hound growling softly at the entrance to the Gate room or even the still missing Sonja O'Dane I sensed. I shuddered to a stop next to Galleytrot and stared at the Sidhe prince waiting in the middle of the room.

Thalion, prince of the Seelie Court, stood on our side of the veil. And he looked very unhappy.

"Your Highness." Thalion bowed to me, speaking to Shaylee, as usual. This time I didn't bother correcting him, taking in his pale features, how drawn and tired he looked, figuring I'd cut the guy some slack.

He looked like he'd been having a bad day.

"What's wrong?" I approached immediately, offering him my hand. Thalion's was cool to the touch, his power sliding over mine, though, for the first time, I didn't get a slimy, needy vibe from him. Neither did Shaylee. Instead, he felt desperate.

"Our realm is under attack," he said. "The storm is rising and we need your help."

The storm. I'd seen it when I crossed last time, a dark and oppressing line of black clouds huddled on the horizon of the Sidhe plane. I'd thought it was partly due to Ameline's interference, the rising thunderstorm rumbling with echoing thunder and lightning flashes. Clearly that wasn't the case. My suspicions about the Brotherhood's involvement made my heart clench in fear.

"Let's go." The Gate already stood open, humming softly, though, as I drew near I heard the faint discord in its song. One look through the veil told me what I needed to know.

The storm had grown all right. So much, it almost covered the entire skyline visible through the doorway.

Thalion led the way, me close behind him, the touch of the bubbled edge of the Sidhe veil as uncomfortable as ever. I stepped through the soapy film, feeling the glamour of the realm try to shift my appearance but, stubbornly refused to give in. Shaylee supported my choice and, though occasionally the hem and skirt of an elaborate dress flickered to life around my feet, I held onto my own shape.

Was it stupid to fly headfirst into the Sidhe's problems when I had my own to worry about? Yeah, probably. Still, the need to do something was much more powerful than my ability to sit on my ass and wait for the world to come crashing down around me. Besides, Shenka had the fort, Sassafras at her side for support. And no one, not even the Council, could fault me for answering a call for help.

I hoped.

I drew in a short breath, the hint of ozone heavy in the air choking me. The sky appeared black to the west, over the realm of the Unseelie, though most of the Seelie court territory seemed to be clear still.

"The king wants to see you." Not the Queen? Who

was he working for these days? Thalion strode off, long legs covering ground quickly as his power compressed the distance. One minute we were hurrying along a stone path up a green hill, Charlotte in blonde wolf form loping at my side, and the next we stood at the border to the Unseelie realm.

King Odhran waited on the other side, his queen, Niamh, beside him, ranks of Unseelie in their odd, often ugly forms assembled behind him. They had created a camp of sorts and I wondered if they'd moved from this place since I left them last time.

An archway formed in green fire, allowing me through. The moment I did, when I left the glamour of Aoilainn's influence and entered Odhran's, I gasped.

The storm. It covered the entire sky. Flashes of lightning and a moaning wind followed by deep, threatening rolls of thunder made me shudder like a child woken from a nightmare to realize the nightmare was real.

Odhran offered one hand, his face as gaunt and drawn as Thalion's, entire body flaring with Sidhe fire.

"Thank you for coming." He followed my gaze as my eyes lifted again to the black mass of clouds hovering like a ceiling over the browning grass on the other side of the border. "Things have not improved since we last met."

"No kidding." I hugged myself and shook my head. "You should have called me sooner." I turned to Thalion who stood beside me. Another shocker. What was he doing on this side of the border? "Since when is a Seelie prince welcome in Unseelie territory?"

Thalion shrugged gracefully even as the queen laughed.

"Since he's made himself valuable," Niamh said. "Trying to convince that stubborn, willful Seelie wench to pay attention and notice her world is crumbling around her."

The queen of the Seelie had proven herself to be less than reasonable.

Shaylee sighed, but held her tongue. I knew it was hard for her to think of her mother that way, but after she'd forced Shaylee to leave me and inhabit a body of foliage that would have weakened and trapped her, leaving her vulnerable to Ameline, I didn't much care what Shaylee thought of her mother.

Considering I had my own mommy issues, we were a great pair.

I looked across the border at the lighter sky, a terrible feeling growing. "The storm?"

Thalion nodded sadly. "My queen does what she can to hide it from us," he said. "But it's consumed the entire sky in the Seelie court as well. Only her powerful glamour keeps my people from knowing what approaches." He paused. Winced. "What has arrived."

"It's no ordinary storm." Odhran repeated the obvious, but when he pointed to the ground, I understood what he meant. A wavering patch of darkness came and went, as though the edges of the very earth decayed under our feet. As he went on, I looked up and around, spotting more and more of these dark patches, eating away at the realm. "It draws power from the veil protecting our plane." He shivered, leaning on Niamh who sent a surge of green fire to him, only to sag herself. "It takes all the will we possess to slow the outflux, but we are weakening. I fear, when we fall, the realm will fall with us."

And they said Aoilainn was stubborn. "You waited this long to tell me?" Of all the stupid, ridiculous, hard-headed—

"We have nowhere else to turn." Odhran bowed his head to me. Had to hurt. The Sidhe were a proud race. "We have done our best to protect our people, but we now know doing so is impossible without your help."

Time to set aside accusations and pride and do something. Right.

"What about Aoilainn?" Shaylee shuddered at the thought her mother could just let this go on without fighting.

"Perhaps if Her Majesty could be convinced to fight back," Thalion said, "we could join forces."

Queen Niamh laughed again. "The Seelie and Unseelie? Join together?"

Odhran shook his head, but not in denial. "It may be

our only hope."

If so, they were totally screwed. I agreed with Niamh. No way would Aoilainn give up her power so easily. Even Shaylee admitted her mother would rather see the realm fall than join forces with the Unseelie.

Which meant there had to be another option.

I stepped away from them, reaching out with my magic, feeling the storm. I should have done it the first time I was here, but I'd had other things to keep me occupied. Like Ameline and losing Shaylee and Liam almost dying. Yeah. But this time I could focus.

The moment my power grazed the edge of the storm I started to swear. Softly, under my breath, hands clenched at my sides, body shaking with the need to hurt someone.

Preferably Liander Belaisle.

Blank emptiness met my magical touch, pulling at my power, trying to suck me dry. I had to jerk free, to call on the depths of the blackness beneath me as the petals of the dark flower of my sorcery parted with a sigh and opened. Answered the call of the storm and began to suction power from the realm.

Oh *hell* no. I put a stop to that immediately, cutting off my sorcery with a layer of creation magic, feeling the maji in me rise and take over. Everything stilled, calmed within me. I'd been practicing, focusing myself on my maji abilities, but they still fought me until I had a task to do.

And then everything seemed to come together.

Like now.

I reached for the storm as my maji power swelled in answer.

chapter eight

No sweat. This would be no sweat whatsoever. I felt myself rise both in spirit and in confidence, my mind and magic flowing upwards toward the edge of the emptiness. Creation power hummed, ready for action. I'd never felt more powerful, more in control of my abilities as I reached out through the blankness, searching for Belaisle and the source of the power draw draining the Sidhe realm.

And tumbled back, falling on my ass in the dying grass as answering magic rippled over the surface of the storm and threw me off.

I stared up in surprise, head ringing, body tingling with the shock of the violent recoil. Charlotte's hands grasped my arms, her human form returned now that we stood in the Unseelie realm. The monarchs of the Unseelie had no power to spare to play dress up.

47

"Thanks." I brushed at the seat of my jeans, face so tight in a frown my cheeks ached. "Well, that hurt."

Odhran stood mute, watching me. His disappointment looked to be about as powerful as mine.

No way I was letting the Sidhe down.

"Just give me a second." I shuddered off the last of the tingle and gathered my power again. Went more slowly, eased my consciousness closer instead of my typical all or nothing. Ran into the exact same layer of protection against my power.

I examined it for a moment, letting the maji energy slide along it, probing and exploring. There was something familiar about it, but reversed, as though I looked at and felt the underside of a power I knew. No amount of probing or poking could break through, though I came close several times.

Very close. Twice. The first time when my bright creation energy connected with equally bright creation energy. Broke free as blackness sliced through the bond. Tried again, felt the sparkly, happy, brilliant power reach for me. Only to have the darkness snarl and shove me aside.

I sank from the storm, the edge of emptiness, a sick feeling pooling in the pit of my stomach.

I couldn't do this alone.

And there was only one other person who had the powers I did, but was connected to the dark.

No. Freaking. Way.

I was going to need Ameline to save the Sidhe.

Odhran and his queen watched me with weary resolve, their disappointment no longer showing.

"You were our last hope," he said. "But if we are to fall, it is on us." He reached for me, took my hand. "Our thanks for trying."

I couldn't just leave it like this. But no way was I cutting Ameline loose. There had to be another answer.

"Send emissaries to Aoilainn," I said, trying to keep the desperation from my voice. "Thalion, you have to convince her. You need each other." The divide in the realms made them weak. I could feel it, the seam in the storm, drawing on the Sidhe like a leech. Dark and light called to each other here at this level as much as they struggled and combined in the storm above.

Thalion sighed but nodded. "I will do my best."

"I have to go," I said. "But I'll be back. I just have to track someone down and get some answers." Whether she wanted to give them to me or not. And that was only if I could break into the vampire mansion and reach Iepa.

If, if, if.

I left them there, still fighting, resolute and failing and knew if I didn't find an answer, the Sidhe realm would fall.

And the Brotherhood would win.

Charlotte and I crossed back into the Gate room, the

portal sighing shut behind us.

Liam had been pacing, stopped with his hands clasped in front of him, Galleytrot's large eyes flaming red fire as they focused on our return.

"Well?" Liam came toward me, face falling as I grimly shook my head.

"Not good," I said. "I'm working on it."

He nodded quickly. "I'm combing the archive," he said, voice shaking as his hazel eyes sparked with green glints. "But there's nothing, Syd." His strawberry blonde hair stood up in weird angles, the cause apparent as he ran his hands through it for what had to be the millionth time. "Nothing."

I hugged him, whispered some platitudes I don't remember and which did little good before leaving him there to stare at the quiet Gate.

Galleytrot followed Charlotte and I out into the basement hall. I turned to him as he head-butted me.

"We can't let the Sidhe fall," he said.

More people stating the obvious.

"I'm doing my best." I tsked at myself before hugging his big head. "We'll figure it out. We always do."

Until we didn't. When would that day come?

Couldn't think like that.

"I'll talk to Mom." That was going to be a joy and a half. I could just imagine my conversation with my Council magic controlled mother. How the Sidhe were their own people and had nothing to do with witches. Galleytrot didn't seem all that inspired by my statement either. "At the very least, she has to be kept informed."

He shook himself, mane swinging, the scent of a summer storm and crushed fresh grass rising from his coat. "If there is anything to be done," he said in a voice rumbling like thunder, reminding me of the storm I'd just left behind in the realm. "I know you'll find it. Just hurry."

He didn't have to tell me twice.

Charlotte took my hand even as I stretched out mine for hers the moment we exited the side door, a heavy moon hanging overhead. I tore at the veil, distracted, heading for Mom, knowing seeing her in person would be the only way she'd listen.

She wouldn't like it. But I had no choice.

The moment I stepped into the veil, Ahbi Sanghamitra showed me she still had control over me after all, dead or not. Before I could fight her, instead of delivering me across the rubber membrane to Harvard, the Node's power, my demon grandmother fused to it, sliced open the way between planes.

Dumped me out onto polished black stone over a pair of booted feet. On my hands and knees, a growling creature crouched beside me.

I looked up.

And into Meira's startled amber eyes.

"Hi, Syd," my sister said. "What are you doing here?"

CHAPTER NINE

I gaped at Meira for a minute, her demon form taking me by surprise. Not that I didn't grow up with her red-tinted skin, thick, black nails and cute little horns peeking out of her hair, but it had been a while and she was so...

Mature.

Being on Demonicon aged her, took her lovely, sweet features and rounded them up at least a decade, if not more. She looked as old as me, though there were eight years between us. I took her offered hand, a little surprised to see my own was still human.

The dark creature at my side growled again and it was only when I looked down and met its eyes I realized "it" was a "her". Charlotte somehow crossed with me this time, her wolf form turning into an oddly reptilian and altogether vile looking, black-skinned critter with fangs like dagger blades and three jointed back legs giving her an odd squat.

I reached out and touched the top of her knobby head, rough like sandpaper as her giant eyes sparked her fury. "Sorry about this," I said. "No idea how she managed it. We won't be long."

Charlotte's voice was more a cry than a growl, high-pitched and painful.

"You have a tame *rimoranolis*?" I looked up, realized only then Meira wasn't alone. That my grandfather, Henemordonin, was with her. And, at the other end of the table, staring in fascination, sat Theridialis, Sassy's father.

"She's a werewolf," I said. Glanced down at her new form and tried not to shudder. "Well, at home, anyway."

"Fascinating." Theridialis heaved his bulk out of his chair, round belly preceding him as he approached. He hugged me briefly, amber eyes full of questions as he looked me up and down before turning to Charlotte. "Quite remarkable, really."

Right. I was still human. Had to have something to do with my tight hold over my humanity in the Sidhe realm. I relaxed my grip, felt myself stretching out, my skin taking on a red hue, fingernails growing slowly, thickening as my perspective changed from feeling really short to almost being at height with Meira. She wore a pair of her favorite platform boots, giving her a few inches on me and I did my best not to stand on my tiptoes in an effort to be taller.

My demon chuffed softly.

Thanks for letting me out, she sent.

Smartass alter ego.

"I take it you're not here by choice?" Henemordonin crossed his big arms over his wide chest, face furrowing in a frown as his steel gray brows descended in a sharp "V" over his eyes. Poser. Drove me nuts when he did that. But I guess centuries of being a politician embedded certain behaviors.

Still irritating, though.

"Grandmother didn't give me a choice." I'd stopped calling Ahbi that at one point, still thought of her by her given names. But it wouldn't hurt to remind Henemordonin I was his granddaughter.

Ugh.

Theridialis's eyebrows rose. "Your claim our beloved former Ruler lives on inside the Node is still up for debate."

Seriously? Sigh. When would people start believing me for once? "Yeah," I said, "well, debate it with her, would you? I have stuff to do at home and this little side-trip wasn't my idea."

The door at the end of the room opened as I finished. I glanced toward it and felt the little girl inside me who still missed her daddy squee in excitement. Everything fell away, all my worries and fears, as I ran to

Dad and wrapped my arms around him. He hugged me back, lifting me from the ground to swing me around.

"Cupcake," he whispered in my ear.

Sheesh. I'd be an old woman—if that ever happened—and he'd always call me "cupcake".

Funny, I wasn't really upset about it anymore.

Dad set me down and pulled away first, smiling at me though a frown just visible enough I knew he worried. "Nice to see you," he said.

"You too." Couldn't help beaming. Man, I loved my dad. Hard not to let some sadness creep in, knowing he and Mom would never be together again. That being here was the only way I could see him.

Way to ruin the happy daughter moment, Syd.

His eyes went to Charlotte, brows rising to meet his hairline. "Something you want to tell me, Syd?"

It only took a few minutes to let them in on what was happening in the Sidhe realm. Why wasn't I surprised when Dad stopped me part way through with a stunned expression.

"The Brotherhood?" He sank into a chair, pulling me down into the one next to him. "I think you'd better start from your last visit, cupcake."

So odd going back through it all, my first trip to the Sidhe realm, the theft of the Dumont power, the attack of the Brotherhood. Miami and the machine I'd destroyed. Mom's fight with the Council power. I felt a little guilty as I filled them in, glancing sideways at Meira, wondering why she hadn't told Dad already. Knowing, from the look on her face, she had no idea.

And that it really was my responsibility to keep everyone up to date.

Turns out the vampires weren't the only loved ones I neglected.

When I wound down with my worries about the present struggles in the Sidhe realm and my fears about Ameline, Dad sighed and sat back, one big hand pressed to the black stone table, fingers tapping a slow rhythm while my grandfather stood and paced to the large window beside us, staring out with his hands clasped behind his back.

Meira had no trouble meeting my eyes, at least, a far cry from the cold and awkward relationship we'd shared since she'd fallen prey to Sassy's mother and her altered form of nectar. I worried about Meems so much, but here she sat, calm and composed, more poised than I was, every inch a demon princess.

While I felt like a shlump.

Dad finally looked up, eyes troubled while Theridialis rocked in his chair, tapping his chin with one finger. "Things have been quiet," he said. Grinned. "For Demonicon." Yeah, quiet. I bet. "But there have been subtle fluctuations in the Node."

"The monitors explained that," Henemordonin said

without turning around, though, from the tone of his voice, he wasn't buying what they were selling, at least not completely. "The Node is still settling after the incident." What a lovely way to describe the fact Demonicon almost split back into its tiny parts shortly before my demon grandmother's spirit became lodged inside.

Incident. Okay then.

"There's no proof it's Ahbi," Theridialis said before Meira snorted, eyes sparkling, lips turning up into a smile.

"I'm with Syd," she said. "It might not be overt, but every time I use the veil, I feel something." She sat back with her arms crossed over her chest. Holy. Did she have a bigger rack than me?

And was I jealous? At a time like this.

Shallow, Syd. Really damned shallow.

"Regardless," Henemordonin said, turning to face us. "Demonicon is fine. No signs of interference."

Ahbi brought me here for a reason, though, didn't she?

"We need to be on alert." Meira stood, pacing past the end of the table. She'd taken up my favorite habit in times of stress. "If Grandmother brought Syd here, something has to be wrong."

Wow. We were thinking alike now.

Freaky.

And even better—or worse, depending on how I looked at it—as Meira came to a halt, one hand pressed to the table, shoulders back, face set, I realized what the real difference was. Beyond the fact she wasn't angry or sad or bitter anymore.

She fit. This was her place, her world. She looked, acted, felt like she should be here.

Lucky. I wondered if I'd ever feel like I fit anywhere.

The door opened for the second time, a tall, handsome demon closing it quietly behind him before approaching the table. A grin split my face, despite the pressures of home, the nervousness triggered by my unexpected arrival. Rameranselot grinned back before bowing to Dad.

"Ruler," he said. "You summoned me?"

Dad looked confused then nodded. "Sorry, forgot." He gestured at me. "Our visitor has broken my train of thought."

Ram smiled at me again, smirked. Yeah, I missed that smirk, no matter how much it made me want to punch him.

Kiss him.

Punch—

Aw, hell.

"I'll speak to the monitors." Henemordonin looked more troubled than upset, as though he didn't want to believe Ahbi still existed. "Double our protections." He met my eyes. Nodded. "Just in case."

I watched my grandfather sweep from the room,

hoping whatever reason Ahbi had for bringing me here could be solved with doubled protections.

"And I." Theridialis came to me, bent to kiss my cheek. "You've made me consider perhaps my view of the Node, of our planes, is a narrow one. Imagine." He smiled suddenly, patting his wide belly. "Ahbi, still alive and in control." He chuckled. "Wouldn't she just love that?"

Did she ever.

And that left three. Dad stood himself, took my hand, helped me to my feet.

"I have something to take care of," he said. "But keep in touch this time?"

I nodded as he hugged me, squeezing him hard. I'd have to set up some kind of schedule with each of the races so I didn't forget anyone.

Dad left then, though when Ram tried to follow him, Dad winked at me.

"You two take a minute to catch up," he said, before leaving us with Meira.

Ooh. Dads and their matchmaking.

And then, naturally, it was my sister's turn.

"Come see me before you leave," she whispered in my ear as she hugged me, kissing my cheek.

So how did a life and death situation lead to suddenly being alone with a delicious demon who looked at me like I was good to eat? I had the weirdest life.

CHAPTER TEN

He started moving the moment the door closed, my demon rumbling a welcome as he entered my personal space. Ram's handsome face bent over mine, the shine of his horns catching the light from the window, wide lips welcoming me.

What's a little kiss between friends?

Strong hands cupped my face, his mouth covering mine, gentle but hungry at the same time. And my demon—hell, all of us—leaned into him, fingers sliding over the bare skin of his chest where his tight tunic gaped open, showing off the chiseled muscles under his red flesh.

Ram tasted delicious, like honey and cinnamon and heat. I let myself relax into him, trying to picture us together.

Pulled away.

Sigh.

"What are your thoughts on an effigy?" Weak joke, but I was half serious. Like Sebastian, at least Ram wouldn't die on me. Not for a long time, anyway. Except being with me would mean giving up some of his personal safety, tying him for eternity to a statue on my plane.

Not much to ask or anything.

The frown pulling his face into a squint told me I'd thrown him a curve ball.

"Sorry?"

"Never mind." I hugged him quickly before releasing him. "Thanks for kiss. I needed it."

Ram's frown disappeared, a troubled look crossing his face.

"You're not okay," he said.

"Just... stuff at home." Which I really, really had to get back to. I reached for the veil, felt it resist me. What the hell? The touch of Ahbi's spirit was so clear, her intent so vivid, I gasped and stared at Ram.

Wait. I was here... for him? My grandmother brought me across the veil, dumped me here while the Sidhe were in imminent danger, all because Ahbi wanted me to have a demon for a mate?

Was she freaking kidding me? Talk about skewed priorities.

But there was more. Much more. As I let her in, let

her wind her power through mine, I finally understood.

I'd need them. And they'd need me. Sooner, rather than later. The Brotherhood would come and I had to be able to act without worrying about politics.

Which meant having good relationships with everyone involved.

So not about Ram, not really.

I hugged him again. Kissed him gently. "I have to see my sister."

He let me go, watched me leave, and I felt Ahbi's sigh of sadness as I did.

Okay, so maybe it was about Ram for her.

Sheesh.

Charlotte's reptilian form glided along behind me, her freaky three-jointed legs making her bob up and down like a really hideous carnival ride. I couldn't look at her, instead focusing on the corridor in front of me. The door at the end.

The door I knew. Because it was next to the room I'd lived in when I was here on Demonicon.

Meira waited for me, smiling when she greeted me at the entrance to her quarters.

Hugged me tight.

"I missed you so much." The tears in her voice were as powerful as the choking tightness in my throat and chest.

"Meems," I whispered. "Oh, Meems."

We leaned back, smiling at each other, blinking away mutual tears as Ahbi's spirit hugged us both. Meira shivered, looked around in shock only to grin.

"Grandmother."

I nodded. "I think Dad and Henemordonin are in for a bit of a shock when she finally figures out how to take form again." And I had absolutely no doubt it was on my grandmother's agenda.

Like she wasn't powerful enough before. Now she had the very core of Demonicon at her disposal.

"She feels different, though." Meira sighed. "I suppose dying will do that to you."

"Not to mention being bonded to a planet's power source." I rolled my eyes. "Don't worry about Ahbi. She's got it covered."

Meira took my hand, led me to the small divan placed in front of her gaping window. I tried not to look outside, the vision of falling, falling toward the Parade below still haunting me, though it had been ages since our cousins attacked us on the elevator and pushed me to what should have been my death.

"I've wanted so much to see you." Meira looked down, long black lashes fluttering a little before she met my eyes again. Hopeful. With longing. "I've been such an idiot, Syd."

"No way," I said. "Not even a little. We both... went through a lot." Her more than me.

Meira shrugged off my attempt to let it go. "It changed me," she said. "The nectar. For a long time, I hated who I was. Hated everyone, including you." She squeezed my hand. "Mom. Dad. All of it. When Mom sent me to Europe for school, it just made things worse."

I should have checked up on her. Why didn't I check up on—

Meira laughed. "I can see it in your face," she said. "You're beating yourself up over it."

Guilty.

"I snuck home." She sat back, one foot bouncing at the end of her crossed leg. "Talked to Dad. He agreed to let me live here."

"I didn't know." Mom never told me. Then again, Mom and I weren't really talking.

"I've made my choice, Syd." Meira's smile reminded me of the lovely girl I used to know, the kind, gentle and caring girl I adored. But she had a new edge, one I knew she'd need to survive here. Thrive, even. "I'm living here full time, now. Attending to my duties as heir. And I love it."

"Does Mom know?" She had to.

"I asked her not to tell you." Meira looked back over her shoulder, out the window, her beautiful profile so much like Mom in demon form at that moment I felt more tears rise. "I was carrying a lot of crap around. I didn't want you coming after me. Until I worked it out."

"Looks like you did." I felt myself relax as Ahbi's touch rejoiced at our reunion.

Meira laughed. "I did. And kicked some serious demon butt in the process."

Of that I had no doubt.

She was a Hayle, wasn't she?

Meira leaned toward me, finger tips running over my cheek. "It took me some time to hash things out. Mostly through challenging every demon I could." She wrinkled her nose. "Sassafras wouldn't be impressed with me. Most of the time, in the beginning, I wasn't all that elegant about it. But with each battle, I changed. Learned more about myself." She rubbed her thumb and index finger together, a tiny flame bursting into life before dying in a wisp of smoke. "I hated so deeply it took the power I gathered to teach me there were more important things." She laughed. "Funny, right? Most demons would spiral deeper into darkness. But for me, it reminded me who I was and why I was here in the first place."

She felt much stronger, now that I thought about it. And her easy confidence was tied to her extra strength.

"Once I decided I needed to be heir, to take my responsibilities seriously, everything fell into place. And in a way, I have you to thank for that."

Me?

She bit her lower lip before going on, pinpoints of amber light dancing in her eyes as her emotions rose and tinted her power. "Every battle I went into, whether I liked it or not, I thought of you." Her dark curls bobbed as she shook her head. "Most of the time it pissed me off. At least in the beginning. But the further I went, the easier it was to remember how strong you are. To keep asking myself, what would Syd do?"

Holy. I wavered between loving her so much I could barely stand it and worrying I'd given her a really flawed working model to work from. And yet, she seemed to have done all right.

Maybe I didn't suck as a big sister after all.

"I've been waiting to see you." Meira hesitated, looked up through her thick lashes, the girl she was showing up for a moment. "But I was scared. I'd been so cruel to you. I didn't know how you'd take me now that I was different."

I hugged her hard, pressing my cheek to hers. "I'm so proud of you, Meems." My words barely made it from my lips, my throat was so thick with sadness and joy.

Her breath tickled my ear. "I wanted to tell you how much I love you. How much I admire you." She cleared her throat, her own voice rough. "How much I want to be like you."

Holy. "Meems..." I stuttered a few times before being able to go on. "You're amazing all on your own."

"I know." She winked, kissed me. "But I have an equally amazing big sister to look up to. And I'm so grateful."

More hugging. This time I didn't want to let her go. I'd missed her so much, missed just knowing my sister was there, that I could talk to her, have her in my life. A fierce love I'd never felt before surged inside me, passing to her through my demon magic, returned from her in equal measure.

"Whatever you need," Meira said as we finally parted, wiping at one cheek and the moisture there, "whatever, you call me. I'll be there."

"Meems," I said. "Same here."

It was hard to go. Even knowing I had to, that I had a job to do, the Sidhe to save, it was very, very hard to reach for the veil, to leave my sister behind.

As I entered the rubbery membrane, I reached out to Ahbi directly.

Is that what you wanted?

Her happiness filled me with the giggles. She followed with a suggestive image of Ram.

Blushing.

And then, just before I slid free, home again, a warning of feeling rather than words.

To stay in touch. It was only a matter of time before the Brotherhood came calling.

chapter eleven

The cool, dark of the basement welcomed me, Charlotte stepping out beside me into our plane. I immediately felt Gram's touch, knew she was home, felt her summon me to the kitchen.

Only problem? I was aware before I finished the climb to the top of the stairs her trip with Varity didn't go as planned.

Surprising how the first rays of daylight shone in the kitchen window. How easy it was to forget time moved differently both in the Sidhe realm and on Demonicon. I'd lost the entire night to my travels. Odd, I didn't feel tired, not even a little. Knowing there would likely be slim opportunity for sleep in the next day or so, I figured my unusual wakefulness was a good thing.

Gram thudded the lid of the waffle maker so hard the thing bounced. Varity sat, cross-legged and clearly irritated, from the way her magic vibrated at an erratic frequency. She slumped in her seat at the kitchen table while Shenka met my eyes with a little shake of her head. Her magic set out plates and cutlery as Gram grunted her frustration.

"What happened?" What were they up to again? No, seriously. I'd been to two different realms since I left the house and it took me a second to shift back to problem number one.

Gram's right foot, sheathed in a fuzzy purple sock, stomped against the floor tile. A sliver of earth magic, triggered by her act, sent a shudder through the house. "Applegate happened."

Uh-oh. The leader of the European Council should have kept her nose out of it. But that obviously wasn't the case. Which meant Gram was right telling me to stay home.

"Absolutely refused us admission into her territory." Varity looked about ready to shake apart she was so furious. Her lean face pinched even thinner, two furious eyes glaring as energy skipped over her, puffs of smoke rising as it did. "Imagine."

Gram jerked open the machine top and peeled off the first waffle before dumping batter into it and slamming it shut again. "Met us at the border with Enforcers."

Varity's crossed leg bounced with growing violence.

"Not even a sniff of courtesy in that woman."

I felt my own anger rise as they talked back and forth. "This is ridiculous," I said. "And none of her damned business. By witch law."

Gram just scowled at the waffle maker while Varity sighed.

"Technically," she said, "we do need permission. Regardless of our destination. And because Ethie and I are witches and not vampires..." She dropped her foot to the floor, leaning forward with her hands on her knees, expression tight and angry. "Damn her."

"Which means I could go after all." I was a vampire, wasn't I? And officially of the Blood Clan Wilhelm.

Gram whirled, pointing at me with the spatula she held in a death grip, a drip of batter falling to the tile floor with a splat. "You," she snarled, "and I and Varity are going to eat waffles. And then we're going to go see your mother."

Wow. Gram suggesting talking to Mom?

She had to be pissed.

"There's more," I said, taking a seat, rubbing my face with both hands as my mind whirled. The old ladies fixed me with their baleful stares like I'd done something terrible on purpose while Shenka took the plate of waffles from Gram and calmly began to serve breakfast.

Thank the elements for my second. Normalcy felt great right about now.

I forced myself to eat while I talked, telling them about the Sidhe, feeling my desperate need to help the Fey rise again now it hung in the forefront of my mind. Then, shared my little side-trip to Demonicon. Gram tapped her fork against the side of her plate in irritation before nodding sharply.

"I couldn't stand the old bat when she was alive," she said, "but death seems to have given her some sense." Gram jabbed the air with her fork, the tines ringing as she used magic to spray sparks at me. "You and your sister were both looking for butt kickings. With things the way they are, you're going to need her, girl."

Bully. Except, she was right.

Speaking of bullies, once breakfast was over, we packed up ourselves, marched out to the back yard and I did the honors, leaving Shenka behind as we crossed to Harvard. Gram and Varity took the lead, leaving Charlotte and I to trail behind them, shoving their way into the elevator with so much aggression I worried they might bring down the building before stomping into Mom's sitting room where they came face-to-face with Maurice.

Mom's secretary's grumpy and arrogant expression lasted about three seconds, just long enough for the pair of unhappy witches to shove him to one side and barge past him while he fish-lipped, gaping and spluttering. I smiled at him, gave him a happy wave while Charlotte growled low and threatening on the way past.

If only it would be so easy to deal with Mom.

I almost ran into Gram as she and Varity came to a halt in front of Mom's desk and, for a moment, my heart stopped beating.

Mom sat behind it, but it wasn't my mother. Not the woman I knew and loved. She looked even worse than the last time I saw her, face drawn and aged, twenty years added to her sagging skin, her dull eyes that nonetheless flashed with blue fire as we faced her down.

"Why am I not surprised?" She sounded tired, bitter. "I've just heard from Margaret Applegate."

I wanted to go to her, to offer her support, knowing now the Council power was breaking her down. That it wasn't Mom, not really, who refused to help or act. She fought the control of the Council's centuries of habit, law, and stubbornness with her own will, but it was clear to me now, oh so very clear, my mother was losing.

Before Gram or Varity could speak, I pushed past them. Leaned forward and touched her hand across her desk.

"Mom," I whispered. "It's not worth it."

She shuddered, light leaving her eyes.

"This is killing you." I tried to offer her energy, but she pulled away from me, mouth turning down into a scowl so deep the lines in her face cast shadows.

"You two," Mom looked past me, glaring at Gram

and Varity, "tried to illegally enter European territory."

"Since when is it illegal?" Varity was shaking again, voice vibrating with her outrage. "I've been an Enforcer for most of my life, Council Leader, and I've never, ever been denied access to other territories. Ever."

Mom sat back, still scowling. "Times have changed," she said. "And so have the laws. You are no longer permitted to enter another territory without the express permission of both your Council Leader and the Leader of that territory."

Holy crap. What the hell happened to trigger the change?

"I thought we were trying to create openness and union," I said. "Not more separation."

Mom flinched, but not from guilt. Her whole body twitched from it, Council power pooling around her where she sat. "You dare question the laws of your Council?"

Fine. Whatever. I couldn't get through to her that way. So I had to try another.

"Did you know Celeste Oberman is the leader of Sebastian's old blood clan?" I didn't really have a plan, outside of hitting Mom with everything I had. To see if I could somehow shake her—the real her—loose from the death grip of the power she was trying so hard to wield. "Or that the Brotherhood is right now trying to destroy the Sidhe realm?" I wasn't holding out much hope, but I'd tried to reason with her before. Even tried yelling. Smacking her with facts was the only course of action I had left.

Mom twitched again, one hand going to her throat before she choked. "Neither the vampires," she gagged, "nor the Sidhe," her face turned dark red as she struggled to speak—and yes, I had no doubt it was Mom, my mom, choking behind those words, "are any of our business." Mom gasped for air after she finished, sagging in her chair. Thudded both fists down on the arm rests in clear frustration.

But whether it was frustration at us or the fight I know had to be going on inside her that triggered the physical reaction, I had no idea. Though I had a terrible feeling my mother was fading fast and, if nothing was done, she'd soon be lost to the Council power forcing her to do its bidding.

Could I live with that? And what would happen if I took matters into my own hands?

The stake. The pyre. For trying to save my mother.

Couldn't win for losing.

"Miriam." Gram's voice grated as though she fought for emotional control. "This is absolutely ridiculous and you know it." Varity shifted next to my grandmother, face tight but blank. "Where's your sense, girl?"

I watched Mom clutch at her throat again, my chest tight with the need to help her, to do something, before she looked up and met my eyes, completely ignoring the two old witches. "You have been ordered to mind your own business," she said, voice low and deep, roughened by her struggle. "I warn you, Coven Leader, you're very close to breaking laws that will see you burn." Mom writhed in her chair before her hand dropped and she sagged one more time. "Yes, you are part Sidhe, demon and vampire. But you are also a witch, and subject, above all else, to *our* laws. First and foremost, your meddling will be weighed as a coven leader." She wrenched her head to one side, jaw grinding. "Dismissed."

I wanted to protest, and opened my mouth. This couldn't go on. The Council power was going to kill her, in spirit if not in body. But a giant wave of magic rose, a solid wall of pulsing blue shoving me back. Gram, Varity, Charlotte, too, until we were all forced to retreat, leaving Mom behind her desk alone as the door slammed shut in our faces.

chapter twelve

Well, that was productive.

I stood with Gram and Varity in one corner of the Yard, arms crossed, back against a tree as the pair glared at each other. I could tell from the way their faces twitched they were talking among themselves but didn't have the energy to break into the conversation.

When Gram finally spoke out loud, I jumped.

"No," she snarled, clearly continuing where her mental voice left off, "I wasn't aware at the time the Council power had that much influence. Do you think I would have just let Miriam fall into this bottomless pit without support if I'd known?" She blew a gust of air from between her pursed lips. "It wasn't until Miriam attacked Syd I realized just how far this had gone."

Varity's shoulders slumped, hands clenched into a knot in front of her chest. "I've witnessed such influence," she said. "But never on such a level." Her eyes settled on me. "Nor have I seen a Council Leader fight so hard against her own magic."

To protect me. I knew that already. Gram paced in a tight circle before coming to an abrupt halt with a heavy sigh. Her lower lip quivered a moment before she took my hand and squeezed it so hard the bones ground together.

"I'm sorry," she said. "I should have kept a closer eye on Miriam. Should have tried to help her, acted when she came after you in the spring." I shuddered at the memory of Mom's magic striking out at me when I tried to reach for her. "I knew things were escalating, but she's clearly cracked." That was a big statement, coming from Gram.

"Can we free her?" I already knew the answer.

"She would have to choose to step down," Varity said. "And I think we all know now, she's too far gone inside its control to do so willingly."

"Then we continue to work around her." I could see Gram's anxiety shift visibly on her face, feel it through the connection of our hands as her power rippled over mine.

"I can't just write Mom off." Could I?

Charlotte rumbled a low growl while both witches stared at me, mute and frustrated.

Guess I had my answer. And without anyone else to appeal to, I only had one course of action open to me.

The moment I arrived home, I reached for Liam, felt

him leave the cavern so we could speak.

Have you heard from Thalion? It was wishful thinking to consider Aoilainn would have a change of heart, but I was running out of things to hope for and grasped anyway.

Not yet. Liam's power embraced me, the warmth and steadying strength of his earth magic helping to ground me and making Shaylee sigh happily. I really did miss him. But was it his friendship I missed, or his heart? *But I'll keep you posted.* He paused. *Any luck on your end?*

Not so far. I felt his twinge of disappointment, fed by anxiety. *Same deal. I'll let you know the moment I figure out what I'm going to do.*

I released him even as he tried to speak further, cutting him off. Not because I wanted to be cruel or anything, but the absolute disgust I felt, the fact I felt frozen, stuck, unable to act when acting was so very important, was almost too much for me to keep to myself.

And he didn't need that kind of pressure on his shoulders right now. Besides, I suffered best in silence.

I walked into the kitchen to find Varity and Gram whispering to each other, both jerking guiltily as they straightened when I joined them.

I sighed, knowing no matter how much arguing I did, I'd lose. I was enough my grandmother's girl to know she'd do what she wanted regardless.

Because I would. And did.

I went to them, hugging first Gram and then her tall friend.

"Whatever you two are planning," I said, "just be careful."

Gram grinned suddenly and planted a wet kiss on my cheek. "Don't wait up."

The two vanished out the front door while I added another layer of worry to my list.

I was about to reach for Shenka, to fill her in on my latest failure, when another mind touched mine. One I knew so well he was part of me, no matter what happened between us.

Quaid. I sank into my chair, letting the sun from the kitchen window wash over me, warm me. A chill had settled around my soul, fed by my frustration. But his touch helped push it back. Just like always. Even when I was mad at him, even when he was being a major jerkasaurus, Quaid's steady presence and power gave me strength and warmed me to my core.

While I asked myself if I missed Liam's friendship or his heart, I never had to ask that question when it came to Quaid.

No crying. Too much to do.

Sassafras leaped up on the table next to me and I stroked his fur as I spoke with the handsome Enforcer trainee.

Syd. Quaid's power hugged me much as Liam's had, but different. So different. Solid like the earth, sweet like the water, fresh as the air and hot as fire, his spirit magic followed last, whispering his love for me even as my alter egos all reached back.

I guess I wasn't the only one who took strength from being together.

I would have sat there forever, wrapped up in him and he in me, and had we the time, I know the feeling was mutual. But he sighed, pulled back just enough we were apart, but stayed close so I could still feel him with me.

I take it this isn't a social call? I wished. Like my life ever went so smoothly.

Something weird is going on, he sent. *Strange orders coming in for the Enforcer ranks. We're to start patrolling our territory border and not allow foreign witches access.*

So it was a new law, was it, Mom? Talk about fresh. Like, at that second.

Still stank, though.

There's a reason, I sent before telling him everything. Quaid listened, as always, hissing in the appropriate places, his power supporting me even as he fumed. *Quaid, I don't know what to do.* My desperation rose, reached for him, needing him to tell me what next. But his power gently detached from my grasping as he mentally kissed me.

You don't need me, he sent, heart beating with mine,

power linked in perfect proportion and without a trace of bitterness. *You don't need anyone. But I'm here for you, I've told you that before.* How could he say such things to me, be exactly who I needed him to be and yet be the one person I could never have? *Syd, you know what you have to do next. And you're the only person I know brave enough to act and do what's necessary, even though it might mean putting yourself in danger.*

Tears trickled down my cheeks. *Sometimes I worry I won't be strong enough.* So amazing to have someone to tell. To confess my deepest fear. I couldn't think of anyone else I would turn to with such fear. *That I'll fail them, Quaid. What if I fail them?*

You won't, he sent with so much conviction I laughed and wiped at my tears while Sassafras purred and rubbed against me. *You can't. That's just not your nature. And if you do fall, Syd, it won't be a failure. Not yours. It will be theirs.*

Okay then.

Quaid, Sassafras's mental voice gently interjected. *I assume you contacted us for more than just a pep talk and a warning about weird orders?*

The Enforcer trainee shuddered, power tightening around me again. *I'm an idiot,* he sent. *Yes. You have to be careful. Miriam has ordered you are to be watched and guarded at all times.*

Um, what? Just our coven? Not the others? She'd pulled a similar tactic when the Brotherhood attacked in the spring, ordering two pairs of Enforcers to guard over the covens, an order she rescinded once the machine the Brotherhood used to steal the Dumont magic was destroyed and taken into Enforcer custody.

No, Syd, he sent. *Not other covens. Not other leaders. You. Specifically.*

Oh no, she did *not*.

I volunteered for duty, he sent, *but she refused to accept me.* Sorrow and anger tinged his thoughts. *Three sets of two Enforcers just received their orders. They'll be arriving shortly. And Syd, they've been told to keep you from leaving the property.*

She'd placed me under house arrest, had she? We'd just see about that.

For someone who insists on upholding law, Sassafras snarled, *she seems intent on breaking as many as she can.*

Agreed, Quaid sent. *But she's Council Leader.*

And being controlled by that power. I couldn't blame Mom.

But I could blame the centuries of witches who came before her.

I'm not sure how this is supposed to keep us safer, Quaid sent with some sarcasm, *but you're a threat, Coven Leader Hayle. Officially enemy number one.*

Nice to know.

Too bad she was aiming her big guns at the wrong target.

Thanks for the heads up, I sent. Why was I suddenly

feeling more confident instead of less? Almost giddy with anticipation?

Because, my vampire sent, *by forcing your hand, Miriam has freed you to act, given you the motivation you needed to do what you must. And while the coming Enforcers can try, there is no way they can stop you and they know it.*

I felt them arrive at the same moment, the rush of their power heralding their appearance and stood, walking to the door. Still linked with Quaid, I stormed out into my driveway while six Enforcers in plain clothes—suits and sunglasses for goodness sakes—approached the front door.

A wall of magic stopped them in their tracks, the tall Enforcer in the lead bouncing back from it so hard he stumbled and almost fell. I glared, arms crossed over my chest, Sassafras curled around my feet as Charlotte chuffed and snarled beside me.

The lead Enforcer looked like a brick wall, dark hair shaved to a buzz cut, eyes lost behind his mirrored glasses. He looked so much like one of the Brotherhood's sorcerer bullies I reached for him and tested his power as he spoke, just to be safe.

Yup, witch. And arrogant. Hell yeah.

"Coven Leader Hayle," he said, voice rumbling deep. "We've been ordered to contain you in your home until further notice."

"And you are?" I'd dealt with bullies of all races and

he, frankly, wasn't impressing me.

"Enforcer Howermall," he said.

He's powerful, Quaid sent in a warning. *And very good. He and his team are sent in for the toughest cases. Watch yourself around him.*

I think that warning needed to be the other way around.

"First name, jackass." I wasn't taking crap. None.

He hesitated, jaw grinding. "Thomas."

"Okay, Tommy boy," I said while Quaid winced in my head before laughing and commenting quietly on the size of my balls, "listen up. You and your little friends here? You're breaking the law." They all twitched, but didn't move. "You are unwelcome on Hayle property, in Hayle territory, and I'm ordering you to leave. Now."

Howermall shuddered, but shook his head. "We're under our own orders," he said. "The Council Leader's."

Nice one, Quaid sent. *Keep pushing him. It might work.*

Oh, I had every intention of pushing. Hard.

All the way to the edge of my territory.

"Considering covens are autonomous," I said, "her orders have no merit."

Sassafras hissed happily in my mind. *When did you become so clever?*

I was thinking the same thing, Quaid sent.

Great teachers, I sent back.

The Enforcers all twitched again. I could tell they

weren't happy about their assignment. And I was right. The law was the law.

"We have an impasse," Howermall said, voice softening. "But we must remain, coven leader."

Okay, I'm impressed, Quaid sent. *Now, kick him where it hurts.*

Snort. But I couldn't be complacent. I'd won the fight if not the war. "Tell you what," I said. "You can stay. But you're not allowed inside my territory. So, get your Enforcer behinds past the borders of Wilding Springs. And stay there. If you cross into my territory again uninvited, I'll be forced to have you charged with trespassing on a coven's property without due cause." I paused. "Unless you have due cause to contain me, Enforcer?"

He shook his head. "No cause was given," he said.

Mom must have been desperate to go this far.

"Time for you all to leave." I shoved against him with my magic. "Three." Foot tap. "Two." Glare with power flaring. "One—"

He turned, gestured to his people. And they left.

But they didn't go far. I could feel them, as they reappeared outside Wilding Springs, doing their duty while I fought down the surge of rage burning inside me.

I'll do what I can from my end to keep you posted, Quaid sent. *I'm sorry, Syd. I wish I could be there.* His mind clenched in frustration and indecision before his power relaxed and engulfed mine. *I could be.* So soft. So tentative.

You'd be kicked out of training, I sent. *That would mean the end of your chance to be an Enforcer.*

I know. His hesitation didn't last long, but it was long enough.

I'll be fine, I sent, purposely brusque, giving him the out he needed. Knowing I could have had him. But for how long? And at what cost?

I wouldn't be the source of his unhappiness. He'd had way too much of that in his life already.

Quaid left me gently, sadly, but he left. I felt Sassafras's magic hug me in sympathy before sparking in rage as he joined me in reaching for Mom.

Normally she blocked me out. This time, I used maji power to make sure she couldn't, slamming into her, forcing her to hear me.

You've broken the law, Council Leader, I sent. *Careful, or I won't be the one on the stake.*

I shut down our communication, sealing it with sorcery as her power battered furiously against me, trying to get in. Forget it. My vampire was right.

Mom just gave me the motivation I needed to tell the whole world to screw it.

chapter thirteen

I monitored the location of the Enforcers for the rest of the day, keeping a close eye on them just in case. Anything to gather ammunition against Mom so I could have them removed completely.

"Just go to the Council," Shenka said as I paced the kitchen while she fixed lunch. "They have to listen when their own laws are being broken."

"Except they aren't now," Sassafras said. "And with them outside the border, we can work around them while Miriam feels secure Syd is being watched. It's a win-win."

I wished I agreed with him, though, from the sharpness of his tone, I knew he wasn't as happy about the situation as he made out. Still, eggs and omelets—and I'd broken enough eggs in my lifetime I was sick of them for breakfast.

It wasn't until night darkened the sky again, while I

struggled with worry for the Sidhe and my own denial of what I had to do to make things right for them, that I felt the Enforcers stir. The moment I reached out to see what happened to trigger their attention, my rage returned and, with a snarl, I dove out the front door, hitting the street with a jerk on the veil, flashing out in a blaze of power.

The gathered Enforcers spun at the sight of me when I leaped from the other end, magic flaring, as I let all of my alter egos show what they had to offer. The dark flower of my sorcery bloomed as my vampire, Sidhe princess and demon joined my family magic and the iridescent power of the maji.

An old, rust-spotted RV was pulled over to the side of the road, a tall, dark-haired girl's furious expression turning to smug anticipation as I stomped to the edge of my territory.

"Hi, Syd," Trill said. "Are we too late for dinner?"

"Not at all." I copied her casual manner despite the power hovering around me. "Hope chicken casserole is okay."

"Perfect." Trill turned to Howermall who glared back and forth between us. "If you'll step aside," she said. "I don't want to keep the coven leader waiting."

His hesitation told me Mom ordered him not to let anyone with magic come near me. He was lucky a string of three normal's cars drove by at just that moment or he would have found out in intimate detail just what I thought of his pause to reflect on what my mother wanted.

The moment the tail lights of the last car vanished over the hill toward town, I let my anger out, though at least tempered by the moment to contemplate my next action. A show of force was obviously necessary, however, and I felt absolutely within my rights to use it. My snap of power over the edge of the family territory lit up the local patch of sky like the northern lights on steroids. Hopefully the show told him he'd better watch his step.

He got the message loud and clear. Howermall backed down, bowing his head to me. "Coven Leader," he said.

"If you ever," I slashed at the border again, sending waves of magic in a rainbow of colors cascading across it, sparks escaping to hiss on the grass by the side of the road, "ever," this time I sent a rumble of earth magic through the ground under his feet, making him stumble, "ever," a tornado of power whirled around him and his people, jerking on their hair and precious suits, stirring enough dust to make them choke, "try something like this again," the sky darkened overhead as the heavy clouds answered my call, a rumble of thunder echoing in the night, "I promise you, it will be the last time."

He didn't say anything. Just stared, holding my gaze as Trill climbed behind the wheel of the RV and drove it over the border, still staring as I waved her on.

Held his eyes. Until he finally looked away.

Hell yeah.

I sealed the edge of the border with sorcery, much as I had with my power against Mom, tapping against it as Howermall scowled. "I warned you," I said. "Don't push me."

It had to suck, being left there, impotent. Just wasn't feeling the sympathy.

I arrived home after Trill and her family pulled into the driveway with their big camper, partly because I took extra time to examine the four points of power anchoring our family territory. North was already covered, thanks to the Enforcers and their little attempt to control me. East was as strong as ever, even better now that my sorcery fed it. Any magical attempt to break through would draw on the user's own power. I kicked myself as I rode the veil to the west. I should have thought of this ages ago, wondering to myself as I landed in the dark quiet night if it would even work against the Brotherhood.

Not likely. But I still felt better. My eyes settled on the entrance to the cave, the place where I'd first met the vampire essence when she was still trapped in the body of the Firbolg magician, Cesard. Where Ameline fell. Where Sebastian had come to die.

And, on impulse, not sure why I did it, I sealed it, too. Completely this time, with sorcery and maji power. The air around it shuddered, the view of the cavern entrance, a large rock covering it, wavering and vanishing.

Safe. For what? I had no idea.

But I had a terrible feeling I'd be needing a safe haven at some point. And this was the only one around.

A quick trip to the south and I was on my way home. The soft grass of the park gave way under my feet as I crossed into the back yard. And froze.

Charlotte glared at me where she stood near the door. Oh, crap. I'd left her behind in my anger. At least she didn't shake or look like I'd damaged her, not physically. But the hurt on her face, the stern resentment, twisted me up inside far worse than anything else.

"I'm sorry." I reached out for her hand, but she remained rigid, fingers cold in mine. "I really am. I didn't think."

"No," she said. "You didn't." And turned her back on me, going inside.

Sigh.

Temperamental bodywere's with phenomenal guilt skills weren't for the faint of heart.

I followed Charlotte into the kitchen, spotting Shenka's wince first before she hugged me.

She's not happy, Shenka sent.

No kidding.

But my pissed-off bodywere would have to wait, now that my kitchen was packed with Zornovs. I grinned and went to Trill, hugging her tight before turning and squeezing Owen. He'd grown some, the top of his head now level with my nose, but he was as sweet faced and cheery as ever, brilliant eyes always giving me shivers.

The final Zornov opened his arms, winking broadly. "Hey, baby," Trill's older brother Apollo said. "Miss me?"

Made me laugh even while I considered doing something painful and permanent to him.

"Really, Apollo," Trill snapped. "You're such an idiot." She rolled her eyes at me. "I should have left him back at the park with Nona, but we kind of need him."

Two sides of the coin and a center for balance made three. I didn't blame her.

At least she'd figured her stuff out. Came to peace with her need.

Now, if only I could do the same. But just the thought of Ameline gave me an ulcer.

Dinner felt weird, but happy, despite everything. Relief washed through me, having the Zornovs here. At least they understood, had the combined power to stand against the Brotherhood.

Hang on.

"Trill," I said, feeling my heartbeat increase as the excitement of my idea grew. "I need your help." She nodded instantly, Owen perking while Apollo shoveled food into his mouth. But when I finished telling her about the Sidhe and what happened when I tried to cut off the Brotherhood, Trill sadly sighed and sat back from her own dinner.

"I know what you want," she said. "But there are three problems." She held up one slim hand, pulling down her standing index finger. "One, none of us are Sidhe or have Sidhe souls to carry us in safety through the realm." I considered that, knew I could recruit some souls to find homes with them if it was necessary. "Two, if we take on Sidhe souls," okay, she was way ahead of me, "we have no idea how they will affect our power. If they will interfere." True. But only one way to find out. "And three," she dropped her hand, "it won't work."

Grumble, mumble. "Why not?" They were both, weren't they? Light and shadow? That was their purpose, Trill on the side of light, Owen the shadow and their irritating brother between them, the channel.

"All we need is balance," I said. "You three could give me that."

Trill looked down at her hands. "We're no balance for you," she said. "We have maji blood and sorcerer. But you *are* maji, Syd. You need another of your kind and you know it." She met my eyes as I fought the truth yet again. "One of the dark."

Craptastic.

"Tell me about them." Maybe Trill's experience with the dark maji could help me figure out a way to make working with Ameline more palatable.

Not likely, but worth a shot.

Trill leaned in again, toying with her noodles while Apollo helped himself to a second round and Shenka smiled at him behind her hand.

"You're not going to like it." Trill took a sip of water. I knew stalling when I saw it. She finally spoke, voice quiet and deep. "They are like me, like all maji descendants. Born of the blood, of the original maji who created our plane. But they are... different." Sounded like an understatement. "Not all maji had the prosperity of the races they made in mind. Some focused on acquiring power instead."

Familiar scenario. "I guess it makes sense," I said. "Every barrel has bad apples."

Trill leaned forward and took my hand. "There's more," she said. "Because their focus is power, they have goals of their own. Ours, as you know, is to bring balance. Theirs is the same, but through control, rather than freedom."

"Let me guess," I said, unable to keep the wry bitterness from my voice. "They want to rule the world."

"Every world," Trill said.

Typical bad guy crappola. They needed a new song and dance because this one was getting old fast.

"While they intend to take that control for themselves," Trill said, "they've agreed to join forces with old enemies to position themselves more carefully."

Owen made an unhappy face, blue eyes blinking at me. Trill set her napkin aside, one hand on her stomach as though suddenly nauseated. "They fully intend to betray their allies, to make their own grab for domination, but, for now, they work with the Brotherhood."

Oh, that was just all kinds of awesome, wasn't it?

"Which means, if I do free Ameline," I said, my own stomach clenching, cutting off my desire to eat anything ever again, "I'm handing her over to the bad guys. The real bad guys."

Trill shook her head. "I don't think so," she said. "From what I understand, they are waiting for some kind of leader, a power to come. A maji like them. But dark. Syd, I really think if you free Ameline, they will leave their alliance with the Brotherhood. Which will mean two forces, ours and theirs, against our real enemy."

"And that," Apollo said with a smirk, "is what you call a kick ass plan. Ka-pow, sis."

Was he for real?

Trill scowled at her brother. "It's a theory," she said. Met my eyes again. "But I'm certain I'm right."

Sure enough to risk it? I trusted Trill, of course I did.

But this was Ameline we were talking about.

"So, say this is a good idea," I said. "That somehow I am able to free Ameline and we fight the Brotherhood and everything is sunshine and butterflies and unicorns pooping rainbows." Owen snickered at me. "What happens when the war is over and it's us against them?"

Trill didn't say anything, just looked miserable.

Yeah. Thought so.

Bad idea.

"I don't think we have much of a choice," she said. "Can you talk to your mother? Have Ameline released?"

Shenka dropped her fork, the rattling sound making me jump. She smiled apologetically and shrugged. "You met the Enforcers?"

Trill looked back and forth between Shenka and I. "I thought they were there to protect you."

"Not quite." I shoved my plate aside. "Mom isn't exactly herself these days. Or listening to anything resembling reason."

Trill's face fell. "Then we're lost. First, the Sidhe. Then whoever their next target is. Without balance, without the light and the dark, this war is already over."

chapter fourteen

I stared at the dark canopy over my bed while my mind twisted and turned in so many directions I didn't think I'd ever put the jigsaw puzzle of my thoughts back together.

Trill and I went to the Sidhe Gate cavern after dinner to see Liam. She was able to pass through the wards at my side, Charlotte grumbling on my other, but when it came to the Gate, it was as Trill feared. While she could pass through, her power practically vanished as we stepped across the barrier and into the realm

"I can't function here," she said, turning to run one hand over the bubble between worlds, Liam watching from the other side. "And I doubt my brothers could, either. We simply don't have the right kind of power." Her eyes met mine, her face tiny and elfish on this side, reminding me more of a pixie than Sidhe. "And there's no way of knowing what kind of impact we would have. Possibly negative." She shuddered, hugging herself as a breeze rippled over us from the storm, a crack of lightning and a rumble of thunder seeming to agree with her. "Probably negative."

And even Liam kyboshed the idea of making Trill and her siblings Sidhe.

"I hate to admit it," he said, standing very close to me when we crossed back, the warmth of his body so near I wanted to hug him, "but Trill is right. The only way this will work is with another full maji." He led me, reluctant and irritated, to the archive after closing the Gate, Galleytrot panting as he walked beside me, fur warm and spring fragrant under my hand. Liam ushered me to a seat across from his big, elaborately carved desk and set a book in my lap. It weighed more than any book I'd ever held, pressing my legs down into the velvet cushion while Liam sat next to me, Trill leaning in to peek over my shoulder while Galleytrot stood facing me, eyes flickering with red light.

"I can't read it." Okay, so that came out petulant. I think I earned a little attitude, thanks. And it was true. Whatever language this book was written in, none of my alter egos recognized it.

Wait. I was wrong. I had seen it before. In the maji chamber.

"This is the language of the Creator," Liam said. As

always, his voice took on a tone of excitement when he talked about one of his books, even though the message was grim. "It says what Trill's been saying all along. Balance is necessary. And that two maji, one of the shadow and one of the light, will stand against any disaster."

Except freeing Ameline would be a disaster. Of monumental proportions. So monumental, I'd probably have to run for my life after abandoning my family magic.

Hell on a pocket rocket.

I did what any sane-minded woman would do. I ignored them both and went home. Locked myself in my room and sat there for a long time, staring at my reflection in the mirror, begging someone, anyone to come along and tell me, well sheesh, Syd, we're sorry, but here's how you fix it. No Ameline necessary. Didn't mean to worry you like that.

I knew better than to delude myself. Still.

I just didn't think I could convince myself to act.

A peek out the window behind my heavy curtains showed me the Zornovs parked almost in the back yard again, out of sight of the street and tucked away, safe. I felt the Enforcers on my border, still patrolling the edges. The very touch of them drove my temper to spike all over again.

The need to lash out at them was so strong I had to shake myself. Get a grip, Syd. This wasn't their fault, or

Mom's or anyone's, no really. Except the Brotherhood.

And the damned maji who abandoned us to this mess in the first place.

That was better. Aiming my fury at the maji and the Brotherhood made me feel like I had targets worthy of my rage. I took a long, hot shower, letting the sizzle of the water burn away at me, wash free my anger and leave me calm.

At least, that was the plan. So, why then was I lying here, an hour later, still fuming and thinking and tearing myself to pieces?

I missed Sassafras, knowing he was probably out looking around. He took his job of protecting the coven as seriously as Shenka did. Sucked. I could have used his steady purring to put me to sleep.

Finally, weariness caught up with me about midnight and I felt my eyelids sink, my breathing steady, though the spiraling thoughts in my mind didn't still.

I stand in gloom, an empty place, alone. But I know this place, have seen it in a different way, full of witches and demons, vampires and Sidhe, fighting the Brotherhood. The battleground stands vacant, silent, cold. I hug myself, jaw clenching as a bright light forms next to me and she emerges.

The maji Iepa looks the same, if sadder, her lovely face creased with grief, long golden hair hanging over one shoulder as she comes to stand beside me. Her crystal clear eyes, such a light shade of gray they are transparent, sweep over the dull landscape.

I know it. And not just from the battle.

I know it because I've been there.

This is the Enforcer plane. *My stomach lurches, body tense as I spin, looking for the stronghold. But it's nowhere to be seen.*

Iepa nods, sad. It is. *She bows her head.* There is so much to tell you, and yet so much I can't, not yet. *She takes my hand in hers while I start to shake.* And things aren't happening the way I intended.

Well, that's a shame. *I thought I knew what anger was. Nope, not a freaking clue before this moment as I stand there, the maji woman clinging to my hand, telling me she can't give me what I need and that she's screwed up.*

Sydlynn. *Iepa's tears glow on her face, tiny rivers of iridescence.* Please, you must pay attention. *I hate hearing that phrase from her, Gram's favorite.*

I am. *I jerk free of her grip.* You're the one whose mind is wandering. Consider. *I begin ticking off points as Trill had earlier in the night, finding it satisfying for some reason.* The Sidhe are under attack and I can't save them. My mother is being destroyed by the power of the Council and witches she's trying to protect. *Another finger falls.* Dark maji work with the Brotherhood to destroy everything. And you, you tell me I can't have answers. And that things aren't going the way you planned? *A bitter laugh breaks from my chest, tearing at my heart.* Just brilliant.

More tears from her, more grief. I'm trying, please believe me. *She doesn't bother touching me again.* It's taking time to convince the others. That we must act.

The others? The other maji? If they will step up they could handle the Brotherhood, Ameline, all of it. Hope rises, fraying around the edges. Where are they?

She shakes her head, golden hair fanning out around her. They will not listen. But I refuse to stop trying. *Iepa shivers, looking out over the bleakness of the plane again.* I swear to you, I will never stop.

So, no hope after all. I sag, anger draining from me, knowing I have to ask her if what I fear is true, but not wanting to give voice to it.

She saves me the trouble. You must free Ameline. *Iepa nods once, firmly.* While I understand your reluctance, if you are to save the Sidhe, she is your only hope.

Balance. *I bite my bottom lip, soul shriveling at the thought of what I have to do, but finally knowing she's right.*

Can I do it, even with the knowledge? Can I free Ameline?

I just don't know if I have it in me. Even for the safety of the Sidhe. Some things are just too big, too overwhelming to comprehend. Why this is so different, I don't know. Usually, I would simply do what needs to be done and deal with the consequences later.

Not this time.

You must help her develop her power. *Iepa flinches from my flare of fury.* I have to what? Teach her as you have learned. When the time comes, you must both be ready and you will need each other in the end.

Every single part of me rejects what she's saying. Fights her, fights my logical mind.

This can't be. Can't. I'll never believe it, never accept.

And yet, I must. For the sake of my plane and all the others. With one last burst of rage burning through me, I back away. No. I've managed before. Iepa is following some rules of her own. And I work outside the rules. I make my own when it suits me.

This time will be no different.

I leave her there, Iepa staring over the future of our desolation, of the war we have to win, coming back to myself with my resolve firmly in place.

Ameline stays where she is.

I'll find another way.

I opened my eyes, teeth gritted as I sat up.

Gasped as a pale, once beloved face flashed into being inches from my nose.

"Syd," Alison breathed, the musty air from her lungs real, tangible, as her ghostly echo settled in front of me. "I've waited so long for this."

Fangs bared, a light of insanity in her eyes, my former cheergirl bestie lunged right for me.

chapter fifteen

My body thudded hard against the floor as I pushed sideways, pajama bottoms slipping over the sheets. Alison's ghostly form impacted the wall behind my pillow before she spun with a snarl, diving for me.

Fear spiked, adrenaline gushing rivers through my system as I shoved myself back, bare feet scrabbling against the carpet as my vampire roared in fury and threw herself into control of my body.

Everything turned white, glowing, as the essence of the undead extended my hands, a solid shield of spirit energy forming between me and the descending echo. Alison struck it with a cry of pain, bouncing back to hover, crouched on the edge of my bed like a cat waiting to pounce while I scrambled to my feet, vampire spirit magic still firmly between us.

She bared her teeth again, snarling, and I understood.

"You were going to feed on me." I breathed the truth into the cold air, my room chilled by her presence and by the weight of the spirit magic my vampire used to hold her back.

"How do you know I haven't already?" The Alison who never should have been cackled her insanity, head tilting sideways, white hair spilling over her shoulders as her once blue eyes glowed with eerie light. "You sleep so pretty."

No, my vampire sent, firm and fierce as my disgust and fear rose. *I would know if she had.*

I'd take that bit of reassurance, thanks. Cling to it like a lifeline as I shook and tried to gather my thoughts.

We have to capture her. My vampire wasn't just talking to me now as my demon and Shaylee both listened intently. *She can't be allowed to escape again now that she's shown herself.*

I'd thought her passed over, hoped that was the case. Knew I deluded myself thinking so. She took enough of the vampire essence the two times she attacked me, she was becoming something else. Something not quite ghost, not quite vampire. But from the way she licked her lips, stepped down from the bed and slowly circled me, a predator looking for an opening, I knew the blood she'd tasted gave her a hunger for more.

I should have destroyed her long ago. This was my fault. And my vampire was right. I had to do something about it.

The black blossom of my sorcery opened, humming, begging to feed. And while I knew it was probably the safest way, I couldn't bring myself to do that to Alison.

She didn't have the same compunctions. "This is your fault," she snarled. "All of it. If you hadn't come to Wilding Springs, I'd still be alive, still be whole."

Not really fair. "You killed yourself." I felt my vampire reach for her, slow and insidious, the touch of my other powers backing her up. I didn't know what she had planned, but I trusted her to act while I kept Alison occupied.

Not Al. No. Think of her as an echo, Syd.

Make it easier to kill her.

"You did this to me." Alison slapped her chest with both hands, the glow of her stolen spirit magic flaring. "I was popular. Rich. I had everything. And then you had to go and ruin it, didn't you?"

"You were my friend." She shuddered as my vampire's magic reached her, jerked away.

"I wasn't," she snapped. "You really think someone like me would be friends with someone like you?" Her laughter cackled through my room as someone pounded on my door. I sealed it shut with magic, not wanting Alison to escape, and definitely not wanting Shenka in here with me.

Not until the echo was gone.

"You did something to me," Alison said, whining

voice falling into sadness. "That day in the bathroom, when you challenged me. You changed me, used your magic on me."

I did no such thing.

Did I?

My mind flashed back years, to being bullied, to standing up against Alison in the bathroom at school, telling her how sorry I felt for her while her supporters abandoned her and I won.

I won, damn it. And I didn't use magic.

Doubt whispered. I wasn't in full control back then. Magic leaked out all over the place all the time, especially when I was under stress. But I couldn't have used power on her, would have known it.

Did I?

"Thanks to that day," she spat at me while Shenka's voice was joined by Charlotte's, by Sassy's on the other side of the door, "I was broken. Different. I fought it, I wanted to be me." She squeezed her hands against her chest. "I wanted to go back, but I couldn't. And knowing I wasn't me, that I became some alternate Alison you wanted me to be, drove me crazy." She laughed, high-pitched and hysterical even as she lunged, bouncing from my shield again. "You did this, Syd. You. I died because I couldn't live with what you made me."

Holy. No. No, it couldn't be true, I loved Al, she loved me. We were best—

She's distracting you, my vampire growled. *And, through you, us. She's lying. Using your weakness against you. You know it. Now focus.*

I opened my mouth to deny her, to tell Alison she was wrong, had to be wrong, when a calm lassitude washed over me. She smiled, looking more like herself than ever, one hand extended.

"I'm sorry," she said. "Of course it's not true. I need you, Syd. Can we be besties again?"

I wanted that, more than anything. Tears welled in my eyes, spilled over my cheeks, a happy feeling of needing her overwhelming me. And, as she drifted closer, I felt my hold on the shield slip, heard my vampire crying out to me, felt her bite me deep inside. Jerked from the pain, lunged just in time as Alison, her coercion attempt failed, dove on top of me, carrying me to the floor.

Memories of fangs in my throat, of Batsheva Moromond, being drained, fleeing into the veil, left for dead in a mummy state, trapped in the dark... I shuddered, slamming all of the power I had into Alison.

She held on, my magic slipping through her, parts of her wavering and insubstantial, though her claws cut the skin of my arms where she held me. Again I lashed at her, maji power slicing, but she just laughed at me, body reforming, teeth descending.

"That all you got, Hayle?" She whispered against my skin as I realized in panic my magic wouldn't work against her. "My turn."

I felt the air of the room shift just as the first prickle of her teeth touched my flesh, the black, blooming flower beneath me gaping wide in a surge of welcome as someone triggered sorcery just past Alison's ghostly shoulder.

She shrieked, pulled away from me, spinning to hiss at Demetrius Strong who lunged through a circle of black, arm extended, crystal aimed at her, a grim smile on his scarred face.

I reached for her with my own sorcery even as Alison howled her fury and vanished.

Gasping, clutching at my neck, though she hadn't drawn blood, I dropped the shielding around my door, allowing the desperate people on the other side to finally enter. Stupid, I should have allowed them through when I realized I'd lost.

And I'd better believe I'd be hearing just that from the three furious faces glaring at me.

They didn't get to dive into chastisement, not while Demetrius trembled, coming to help me to my feet, clutching at my hand.

"They own her," he whispered, the former leader of the Chosen of the Light now my only ally with a connection to the bad guys.

Wait a second. What had he—Oh no.

No.

"The Brotherhood?" I was having trouble breathing.

He bobbed a nod, bright blue eyes wide and shining. "They captured her," he said. "Tortured her. For information. For things she knows about you." He shivered. "About all of you."

I swallowed hard as the next level of guilt settled around me like a weight. "She's almost real." Not quite. I looked down at the welts on my arms where her claws nearly broke the skin. "My magic went right through her."

Some kind of hybrid, my vampire sighed. *I feared this would happen.*

"You must destroy her." Demetrius's shivering didn't quit, sending vibrations through me thanks to his grip on my hand. "Abomination."

"How did she get in?" Shenka's voice sounded calm, though she looked pale, her dark skin gray with worry. "This place is tighter than a bullfrog's back end."

Demetrius shrugged. "Sorcery," he said.

"They sent her." Had to be the Brotherhood. "But why now? Why tonight?" Distraction?

Again he shrugged. "They need something from you," he said. "Tasty treat, that Sydlynn Hayle." His big eyes rolled around as he slipped further from coherence and deeper into his damaged mind.

"Demetrius." I pulled my hand free, gripping his arms, shaking him ever so slightly. His gaze refocused as I spoke. "Can she become real? All the way?"

A soft whine escaped him, Charlotte twisting her head and wincing as her wolf senses went on overload.

"Mustn't," he said. "No balance."

Hang on. "Alison is part of the balance?" How was that possible?

"She's an unknown." He snapped into lucidity as though he'd never lost it. "A wild card. While you and Ameline are necessary, there is a part of Alison connected to you, to sorcery, to the maji through blood magic. The Brotherhood want it to happen. Consider it important. Which means we must oppose it." He flinched, shook like a rag doll, collapsed against me. "But, more immediate, she is a weapon," he whispered. "If she becomes real, she will be a tool against the vampires, unkillable because, unlike them, she's already been dead. Not just undead." He looked up, grinned like it was funny as I lost him to insanity again. Giggled. "Now isn't that special, jiggity jig?"

Another lost soul come full circle. I had to go after Alison.

Demetrius had another idea. He held up his crystal, jabbed it at me. "I'll catch her, just you wait." He dodged back from me, grinning like he'd lost another pair of marbles from his dwindling collection. "Been tracking her, haven't I? Be right back, don't you know." The air around him shimmered before going black, oozing around to envelop him before he waved and vanished.

Chapter Sixteen

The kitchen filled with the aroma of pancakes, soft talk in the late night/very early morning, the sky nowhere close to hinting at dawn. Gram wielded her favorite spatula like a weapon as Charlotte hovered by the door, staring out into the dark. Shenka squeezed my shoulder as she went about her usual business and I realized then, we'd made ourselves an oddly organized and predictable family. With a routine. I felt like the 50s dad who sat around while life went on without him, waiting to be served.

Charlotte's low growl and subsequent reach for the door made me tense, only to relax as she pulled it open to reveal a yawning Trill.

"Felt a disturbance in the house," she said. "I take it something happened?"

She listened quietly, helping herself to pancakes as I

told her about Alison. I sighed. One more thing to worry about, one more loose thread I let fall and fray because I forgot or was distracted by other things.

"You need to let Demetrius take care of that echo." Gram slammed my plate down in front of me personally, glaring with her faded blue eyes. "We have bigger things to worry about."

Like saving the Sidhe. I'd been hoping something new would come to me, but all I could think of was Ameline.

Right. I had more to tell them.

I spilled the beans on the visit from Iepa while Gram swore around a mouthful of breakfast, Sassafras's tail thrashing so hard he dipped the tip of it in my syrup, a trail of sticky mess painting the table top as he thrashed back the other way, spraying Charlotte with a fine mist of maple.

"I don't trust this maji," he snarled, chin white with a bead of milk he swiped away with one paw as Charlotte glared at him, carefully dabbing the gooey mess from her cheek. "She seems to only show when it's convenient for her and never with the kind of information you could really use."

Trill wiped her lips with her napkin before shaking her head. "No," she said, "Iepa might be many things, but she's trustworthy." Her grimace told me there was a lot she hadn't shared yet.

"Evidence?" Trill, I trusted.

"She saved me, saved all of us, my brothers and I." Trill's hand vibrated with a soft tremor. "When she wasn't supposed to interfere. The maji punished her for it, but she helped us anyway." Tears stood in her eyes, thickened her voice. "So, I believe in her, Syd. That she has our backs. Even when it doesn't seem like she does."

I could have prodded her for more info, but what would be the point? She didn't seem all that willing to talk about it and I wasn't sure it would make me feel better anyway. Besides, there were things she didn't know, nitty-gritties I had yet to share. Figured we'd have time to exchange full-scale war stories maybe when we were old.

Oh, right. I wasn't going to grow old.

I knew for most people the idea of living forever wasn't a bummer, but I couldn't help thinking differently.

Gram thudded both fists on the table, grim scowl pulling at the deep lines around her mouth. "Damn the maji," she snapped. "Damn the fates." She crossed her arms over her chest, thin nightgown strap falling from one narrow shoulder as she kicked me with her bobbing foot. "And damn Ameline Benoit." She stared at me, chin tucked low, gaze dark under her lashes. "If only it was that easy, saying damn them all."

If only. I'd take it.

Or would I? Sucker for punishment.

"If freeing Ameline means saving the Sidhe and defeating the Brotherhood," Gram said the unthinkable before I could stop her, "then that's what you have to do."

No nonsense. No second guessing. No doubt.

I wished.

"I agree with Ethpeal." Trill's voice carried, despite the low, softness of her words. "I don't know how to help you, to keep you safe, but if there is anything I can do, just ask." She met my eyes with her dark brown ones, almost black in the early morning. The white light over the stove glowed behind her, lighting her black hair with frost. "But like Owen, Apollo and I, there must be balance between the light and the shadow for you and Ameline."

"She will fight for the dark maji." How could I just set her loose? Maybe I could control her somehow, keep her prisoner myself?

"She will," Trill nodded, no trace of doubt on her face. "And they will embrace her. I believe that is the key, Syd. She will release them from their ties to the Brotherhood, steer them back on the path they were meant to take so both sides can rally to attack our real enemy."

"And the army?" That would make me feel better. Trill's maji army. Who knew how many maji blood were left and what they would look like coming together? She'd been tasked with gathering them and I felt badly I didn't ask her how she was getting along with that.

But the gentle, almost loving, smile on her face made me pause.

"Syd," she said, voice full of happiness, "there is no army. I misunderstood. It's not the ranks of the blooded we need."

"Then who?" I was so sick of these riddles, half-truths, being led around by the nose, a straight-forward answer would be nice for once.

"You," she said. "You are my army. The souls of the maji bloodline all lead back to you."

ChApTER SEVENTEEN

I retreated from the table, leaving them to talk, needing to escape, to spend some time alone. Especially after Trill's little reveal about me.

A one-woman army. One maji?

Whatever.

As I settled cross-legged in the center of the pentagram, hoping the family magic would keep me safe if Alison made a comeback, a familiar furry form rubbed against me. Sassafras climbed into the hollow my legs made. I stroked his silver body, hearing his purr begin, but softly, without the push of magic behind it.

We reached for the veil together, as though we thought of it at the same moment, tearing open the way between planes until my sister's magic reached back. Meira sat at a desk, watching us through the veil between worlds, large window behind her showing the multiple suns of Demonicon glowing, a frown of worry on her face.

"Are you all right?" She stood, approached the gash between planes. "Should I come through?"

The touch of Ahbi's spirit flowed around me before retreating back to the edge of the veil. But it made me smile, enough Meira relaxed and sat again.

"I've just had a bad day," I said. "I wanted to fill you in."

And I did, Sassafras helping, while my sister, so mature, so much more at ease with her position than I was, nodded sagely before sitting again and steepling her hands in front of her.

"Talking to Mom is out of the question, considering what you told me." Meira stared down at the surface of her desk while she pondered.

"Agreed." Sassafras leaned against me, purr now silent. "Miriam's ties to the Council power have rendered her useless to us."

Worse, it made her our enemy. But I didn't say so out loud.

"If I do this," was I really saying what I thought I was saying? "If I free Ameline," shudder, shiver, hell no, "and we deal with the attack on the Sidhe, I could always return her to prison." Could I really? We'd see. But it sounded better than letting her go, even though Iepa and Trill both seemed to think I'd have to. And made the idea of letting her out keep me from the brink of puking over the family pentagram.

Meira's steady gaze held me. "What do you mean, if?"

Sigh.

"You might want to be ready." Funny how I felt more confident telling her than my father. He might be Ruler, but she felt powerful to me, in control of herself. Less like my little sister and more like an equal.

Imagine that.

"I've linked my own magic with that of Grandmother's spirit." Meira let me feel the connection even as Ahbi touched me again, as though offering the same. But I rejected her, gently and she retreated without emotion. This was Meira's role to fill, not mine. "She'll let me know the moment something happens."

I felt suddenly better, found myself smiling even as I mentally fist-pumped. The Brotherhood couldn't have anticipated this. That the former Ruler of Demonicon would now be part of the Node supporting the planes, how her granddaughter would be able to communicate with her.

Had to be an advantage they didn't anticipate.

At least, I told myself so.

"Bet Theridialis and Henemordonin are both having fits," I said. "Proof Ahbi is still with us."

Meira winked. "Why do they have to know?"

Fair enough.

"Please," Meira said, some of her old softness showing as her grin faded, "take care of yourself, Syd. And if it comes down to it, you know you have a place here."

If they arrested me, she meant. Decided to burn me.

Syd. When. Inevitability loomed.

"Thanks," I said. "I'm already working on it."

Meira waved, disappearing as the veil sealed shut. The feeling of Ahbi's power lingered until my side of the veil healed and then she was gone.

Impulse drove me to hug my demon cat to me, rubbing my cheek against the top of his head as he began to purr again.

"I'm screwed no matter what I do, Sass," I said. "If I don't act and the Sidhe fall, it's the beginning of the end."

He twisted until he could look up at me, amber eyes glowing, but keeping silent.

"And if I free Ameline," I said, "the Council will try to kill me for breaking the law."

"Try," he snarled. Sighed. "I know."

I let my shoulders sag, released all of the tension I'd been holding, finally welcomed the family magic pooling beneath where I sat to rise and embrace me. "I think you know where this is going."

He nodded. "You're going to leave the coven and work alone to protect us."

I didn't answer. Didn't have to.

"I would do the same, in your position," he said, suddenly brusque. "However, we need you yet, Sydlynn Hayle. And you need us."

I hugged him. "I'll always need you." When I let him go, both of our eyes swam with moisture. "I won't give up the family magic unless they arrest me. And I'm counting on you to guide Shenka when it happens." Because, frankly, it was inevitable, and we both knew it. I was now on a path, made my choice, I realized. I was about to get up, leave everything I knew to set loose a terrible evil in the hope she really could help me save the world.

"You're leaving the coven to her?" He didn't sound surprised.

"She's the logical choice," I said, a little shocked how calm I felt. But now that the decision was made, I actually did feel better. Confident. Calm. I'd probably do some freaking out later, but for now, I'd take it. "She'll make an excellent leader."

He nodded. "I agree," he said. "Though most seconds wouldn't, you've chosen one who is as happy to be subordinate as she is to take command. Well done."

Fate again? Maybe. I felt the sadness of the family magic as it clung to me, but knew it would support my choice if the time came.

When. I was having real trouble with that word.

I wondered if my length of leadership would be some

kind of record.

Thought of Mia and her crumpled power, her loss of the Dumont magic and shuddered.

Nope.

"Just promise me," he said, "you'll talk to me first before you make your final decision."

"They might not give me a chance," I said. "If I'm in prison, Sass, you won't be able to reach me."

"Please," he said, pupils huge, ears flattening to the side as his whiskers drooped. I'd never heard him so desperate. "Please, trust me."

"Okay." I hugged him again, kissed him gently between his eyes. "Bossy cat."

"Stubborn child." He head-butted me.

A single sob escaped me as my calm cracked just a little. "Sass," I whispered. "Thank you. For everything. For being here for me even when I wanted you to go. For standing by me no matter what. You've always been by my side, and I love you for it."

A soft whine escaped him as he sagged in my lap. "Syd," he choked around a thick voice. "I love you, too." He opened his mouth as though to say more, but shook himself instead. "I'll always be here," he said. "Always."

I rocked him as we hugged again, taking comfort from him as I did as a child. My fondest, oldest memories had Sassafras in them, I realized then, as well as my darkest and most fearful. He was my constant and the thought of walking away from him broke my heart.

The air beside me shuddered as I spun, shaken free of my sadness in a surge of fear, feeling the emptiness of sorcery stirring in the basement even as a black hole gaped and Demetrius ran through.

He fell into a crouch beside me, eyes gaping huge, hands trembling as they grasped at me, pulling me toward him.

"Come," he hissed. "You must. She is there and it is terrible."

"Did you find Alison?" Sassafras hopped down, amber eyes blazing as he watched the shaking sorcerer. I stood, almost welcoming the distraction from my rising grief at what was to come.

"They are in terrible danger." Tears glistened in Demetrius's mad blue eyes. "Terrible. And she's going to ruin everything."

"Who?" I took his shoulders in my hands, squeezed, shook him just a little. "Who is in danger, Demetrius?"

"Your family," he said. "The vampires."

Chapter Eighteen

Sassafras wouldn't let me go off with Demetrius alone, scampering away to raise the alarm even as I hissed at him to come back. Within moments, Gram and Charlotte hovered next to me while Demetrius did a little hopping dance of frustration over the delay.

"Shenka." I met her eyes, saw her bend to scoop up Sassafras whose big amber eyes blinked slowly at me once.

I didn't have to say anything else.

"We'll hold the fort," she said. "And protect the family. No matter what."

Sassy's tail thrashed in agreement.

"Keep an eye on the Enforcers," I said. "They might try to push you. Don't let them."

She grinned, a nasty expression as Sassafras hummed a growl in the back of his throat. "Might be fun," she said. Trill giggled behind her hand before sobering.

"We'll distract them, if necessary." Her dark eyes glittered in the light of the single bulb illuminating the basement. "My brothers and I have had experience with evasion in the past." I just bet. "Good luck."

I could only imagine what kind of distraction Trill had in mind for the Howermall and his people if they decided to invade my territory. And pitied the Enforcers if they pushed their limits.

My family as safe as they could be under the circumstances, I finally held out my hand to Demetrius, the other taking Charlotte's as Gram snatched the small sorcerer's arm in an iron grip.

He brightened immediately. "Quick!" A gaping black hole opened beside him, the pull of his sorcery calling to the blossom of power at the base of my own magic, the petals sighing open in answer. I squashed them closed, preferring to rely on his power, not sure how ours would blend together.

Okay, that wasn't it. I still feared giving my sorcery free rein and was totally fine letting Demetrius lead the way.

Demetrius said my family vampires were in danger. I didn't need him to explain who he meant. My heart constricted in worry for Sunny and Uncle Frank as I stepped into the darkness and allowed the emptiness to swallow me.

Wouldn't have, had I known what to expect. Would have ridden the veil, avoided the black at all costs. But I had no idea, none. So different, this way of travel. I thought it would feel like the veil, that rubbery feeling, or soap bubbly as happened when I crossed to the Sidhe realm. But this emptiness was nothing like I was used to. Darkness, deeper and emptier than I'd ever felt, devoured sight, sound, touch, taste, smell. All feeling, all magic, everything.

Gone.

I could feel a scream build in my chest, rising from the deepest core of me, denying the loss of self. The emptiness clawed at my soul, took everything I valued and loved, chewed at my sanity while wanting more.

More.

More—

I gasped a breath as I staggered from the black, stumbling with hands outstretched, scream still threatening, into a dark stone hallway. A tiny meep escaped before I could muzzle my aching terror. My shaking hands settled on my weak knees as I bent in half, panting to catch my breath.

Horrible. Just. Freaking. Horrible.

A hand reached for my arm, tugged on me, Demetrius's feet pattering beside me as he danced with impatience. "Come," he said.

I looked up through tears hovering in my vision and

lunged for him, grasping his shirt in one hand as my rage, my demon howling her fury, slammed into me.

"Don't." I choked out that one word. "Don't ever." Pant. "Do that again."

His eyes drooped, sadness on his face. "It ate you," he said.

Shudder. "Is that what happened to you, Demetrius?" My demon retreated to stomp and grumble and throw a hissy fit in the back of my mind as I seized control again and released him. My fingers smoothed the wrinkles in his food and filth spotted t-shirt, left behind by my fist, as he bobbed back and forth from foot to foot, an eerie whine rising from him.

"Eats everything," he whispered so loudly I'm sure they heard him back home.

Because we weren't home anymore. Not by a long shot. And though the mountains I spotted outside the window loomed cold and unwelcoming, I knew this hallway. Had been here before. One look through the narrow doorway into the room next to me and I had my confirmation.

A huge portrait of an unsmiling Sunny looked down on me from the darkness, her gorgeous face lit with the beam of light allowed in through the open doorway coming from the hall.

Why did I feel like she judged me?

"Girl." Gram grasped my hand, her own shaking

slightly as her eyes met mine. From the anxiety in her face, how pale she seemed, she'd suffered the same discomfort I had, though she seemed calmer about it. "We're on splintering glass. Tread carefully."

"Margaret Applegate can bite me." I cared less what the European Council Leader thought at this point. Especially if Demetrius was right, if Sunny and Uncle Frank were in trouble. And I had no reason to doubt him.

A glance at Charlotte told me she wasn't happy either. Her wolf stood in her eyes, coming through in her face as her features morphed slightly into canine shape, though, as I watched, she regained control and nodded once. Her jaw remained clenched, though, skin as pale as Gram's just beginning to take on the flush of life again.

"Hurry, dawn will come soon. We don't have much time." Demetrius's dance increased in pace.

But dawn was hours aw—

Time zones, Syd. Duh.

Demetrius tugged and I finally responded, following close beside him as he moved silently down the red carpet, eyes darting from side to side as though expecting some kind of attack.

Which made me even more concerned. Uncle Frank and Sunny would never hurt me.

If that was true, why was Demetrius so nervous?

Just in case, I opened to my vampire. *Think we should take some precautions?*

She felt as troubled as I was. *Wise*, she sent as she pushed outward, her power shielding the others with her essence. *But perhaps will simply alert the Queen sooner of our presence.*

Hmm. She was right. Six of one problem, half a dozen of trouble.

"Demetrius." He twitched when I said his name. "Alison is here?"

He bobbed a nod, still tugging on me despite our forward motion. "She is," he whispered. "She wants to feed."

On vampires?

That actually makes sense, my vampire sent, her power swirling, making me queasy. *She feeds on creation magic, on blood. Vampires need it to survive. But because she has part of me inside her, it's possible she requires creation energy already absorbed by the undead. What better source than the pure spirit energy of those with whom she shares kinship?*

I mulled that over, still feeling sick, when Demetrius suddenly stopped, even as Charlotte growled like a cornered dog.

"Sydlynn Hayle." I knew his voice, turned to find Piotr Wilhelm, former lieutenant to the original queen and not my biggest fan, standing behind us. Smiling and glaring at the same time, dark hair perfectly styled, tall, lean body dressed in the finest Victorian apparel.

And he wasn't alone. A dozen vampires lined the hall,

more appearing in front of us as I turned my head to watch them flicker from shadow, a gathering from the past like some freakshow theatre production gone horribly wrong.

Not good. "Hi, Pete." I decided on casual, figuring he had us but unable to resist prodding him. "Is Sunny home?"

His grin turned to a scowl, spirit power flaring around him, brightening the hall as the other vampires followed with their own light show.

"Invader," he snarled. "My queen will punish you for your trespass." He licked his lips slowly, fangs showing. "And I will petition her to allow me to drain you personally." His smile widened. "You were so delicious the first time."

Sick bastard. I already guessed he'd tasted my blood, was certain long before now he'd been there when Batsheva ordered me killed. No way was he getting another drop.

"We'll see," I said. Shrugged. I was all out of nice. "Well? What are you waiting for, flunky boy? Lead us to Sunny."

Girl, Gram sent. *You might be invincible, but the rest of us aren't.* Despite her admonishment, Gram's faded blue eyes sparkled as she met my gaze.

I was forced to turn away from her, to face Piotr as he glided forward, in my space, in my face. His breath stank of too much wine and decay as he breathed on me.

"This time," he said, "you will stay dead."

Piotr brushed past me, striding off as the vampire gang approached in a menacing half circle. With no choice, and knowing I had to get to the bottom of this, I turned and played follow the leader.

Chapter Nineteen

Memories flooded me as I made that walk, of being a prisoner of the vampire queens. Forced to choose Batsheva's clan, to become a member, to take her fangs in my neck in order to survive. And almost dying anyway because I didn't learn how to live the games the two families seemed to adore.

I felt my shoulders bunch as I walked. Had to force them down from around my ears, to breathe and stay calm despite the fight between rising anger and the absolute need to turn and run. I could only guess from Piotr's attitude toward me, something changed with Sunny. Either that or, like with Sebastian, she'd somehow been deposed. The very real possibility I was walking into a throne room ruled by a new queen suddenly made me feel so nauseated I had to bite my lower lip hard enough it bled inside my mouth to keep from freaking the hell out.

My vampire remained silent, as wound up as I was despite her usual stoicism. Charlotte's almost constant chuffing behind me didn't help much. My only real saving grace was Gram, grim faced and surly, marching beside me in her thin cotton dress, hip-length pink cardigan and fuzzy orange socks.

I'd built myself up to a fever pitch of Oh My Swearword by the time we reached the end of the hall and the throne room entry. It wasn't until we passed through the archway and into the giant room and I looked up at the stunning blonde on the throne I felt my bundle of fear and fury unclench a little.

Sunny. It was Sunny, absolutely, without question. And Uncle Frank stood beside her. Both of them looked fantastic, a pair of lovers straight from history, she in her ball gown and he in his frock coat and knee-high boots. The giant stained glass window behind them cast an eerie rainbow over them as I strode with growing confidence to the foot of the dais.

That confidence died when I stopped, eyes locked on Sunny's.

She stared with cold contempt, eyes blocks of brilliant blue, flawless face held in a stern scowl that did nothing to shatter her perfection.

"How dare you?" Her voice rang through the room, making her gathered people sway in response. It wasn't until then I noticed how many assembled, I was so focused on her and my uncle. But we were surrounded now, vampires pressing close, hissing and flickering with power, in and out of shadow as they shifted positions. "Invaders. Trespassers! You have come to my home without permission and now your lives are forfeit."

Um, what the hell? "Sunny." I felt myself deflate, emotions failing me, no anger from my demon either. She just gaped, mouth open. And no rumble of an earthquake from Shaylee who gasped in shock. Not even a breath of protection from my vampire who sighed sadly and retreated as though hurt.

"You will address her as Your Majesty." Piotr's voice hissed in my ear, over my shoulder as his bumped me.

Jerktard.

Sunny's scowl didn't waver. "You are here without cause," she said. "And thus, as a vampire of my family, while under my roof, you are subject to my laws. And I order your death for your intrusion."

She had to be freaking kidding me. "Uncle Frank." One of them had to listen to reason.

He swayed slightly, but his hand tightened on the back of her throne as he turned his face away. "My queen speaks," he said. "All obey."

This was not what I expected, not even close. *Gram*, I sent, feeling desperation rise. *What the hell is wrong with them?*

She jabbed me with her power. *Like I'm supposed to know?* She sighed heavily in my head. *The Brotherhood?*

My vampire's magic slipped forward, touching Sunny's, relinking me to the blood clan. I'd done my best to sever my connection, not to hurt Sunny's feelings, but because I had things I needed to do that were none of the clan's concern. But since she made me one of them, I had two choices: reject the connection completely or just put up a wall around it. Since I loved Sunny and thought maybe continuing the relationship might be necessary at some point, I simply did the latter.

Now that the wall was down, my vampire back in touch with the clan, I felt the pull of Sunny's power as she stood in a rush of swishing satin, rage rising on her pale face.

"You dare attack me!" Sunny strode down two steps, almost in my face, her mouth gaping wide as her teeth grew in length, jutting from her pink lips in long, shining fangs, eyes pits of black rimmed in white as she howled her anger.

If touching her power, rekindling mine was an attack, she had a pretty skewed view of things. This wasn't my Sunny, couldn't be, and yet, it was. I had no choice but to protect us despite knowing it would be seen as a threat, wrapping myself in energy. My magic rose, forming a shield around Gram and Charlotte, pulling Demetrius close by a firm grip on his arm, though I was certain he could take care of himself.

"I dare come in front of my queen," I said. "You already admit I'm a part of this family. I have every right to be here."

Sunny's rage flared brighter as she pointed at me with a slashing claw, grown thick and white from her fingertips. "Come," she snarled, the pressure of my blood tie to her activated at last. "Kneel before me and die."

It was there, the pain I remembered, but not as powerful. Not even close to the searing agony I'd felt under Batsheva's orders. The way my insides had seemed to turn on themselves. Yes, it hurt, like bloody murder. But, as I stood there, facing Sunny down, the pull weakened, the jagged hurt lessening until I was able to gasp a breath and shake my head as my maji power formed around me.

"I'm a part of your clan," I said. "But you don't own me, Wilhelm Queen. If you want my blood, you come down here and fight me for it."

I know she would have. Watched her bunch herself even as I pushed the others behind me, to dubious safety. But Sunny didn't get the chance. The moment she shifted her weight to pounce, Alison rippled into being and leaped on the vampire queen with a cackle of joy, mouth locking on Sunny's neck.

I didn't move fast enough to stop Demetrius as he lunged forward with his crystal in his hand. But he staggered, Piotr landing on his back in what had to be a misguided attempt to save his queen from further harm, sending the small sorcerer sprawling on the steps, his precious crystal bouncing away a few feet.

Maji power crackled around me as I lashed out at Alison, wishing I'd brought my own crystal with me, the opening of my sorcery pulling against my other magicks, linking them together. Sunny fought the echo of my old friend, crashing to her side as the ghostly remains of Alison drank her blood. Uncle Frank tackled the pair of them even as my iridescent power sliced through Alison, distracting her long enough Sunny was able to shake the girl's echo free.

Alison met my eyes, her mouth sheathed in red, a cackling laugh carrying in the air as she vanished in a flash of light.

The vampires went nuts, slamming against my shields, trying to reach us as Uncle Frank helped Sunny rise. She stared at me with so much hate, one hand clamped to the gash in her throat, I knew the ghost of my old bestie just made things a million times worse.

"You think to defeat me so easily?" Sunny pushed Uncle Frank away, body morphing as the vampire inside her took over, skin translucent, claws the length of knives, her face dominated by a jaw full of very scary teeth even as her body thinned and lengthened, a deadly skeleton focused on me.

Feel it, my vampire sent in a jab as sharp as Sunny's claws just as the vampire queen launched herself at me. I blocked Sunny with creation magic, knocking her back to crash into the stairs where she scrambled to her feet, hissing and snarling like an animal. But I wasn't paying attention to her, not on the outside.

Not while her inside seethed with taint.

It's been there for centuries, my vampire sent as Sunny threw herself at me again. *Soiling the purity of our spirit magic.* I felt the shielding repel her like a physical thing, endured the hammering of her vampires against the wards I held. For how long, I had no idea, sweat beading out on my forehead. One opponent I could block. But hundreds? Gram's hand settled in mine on one side, Demetrius's on the other, but I kept them in reserve.

For now.

What happened to the taint? My vampire let me feel it before, back when she first emerged. The big difference between her and the undead souls who had come from her. It had never been so black, an oozing layer like oil on a pond, scumming up the feeling of Sunny, blocking out her glow.

I don't know, my vampire sent. *But it's the reason for her loss of self. We must break its hold or she is lost. They all are.*

No way was I going to allow that to happen. I had to save Sunny and Uncle Frank. He had the taint, too, as my vampire traced back through Sunny's connection to my uncle. Dark and fetid, like a slow growing decay, feeding on their creation power, turning it, twisting it into something devouring them from the inside out.

And Alison fed on it.

Lovely.

This has to be the Brotherhood. Made total sense to me. And drove my fear spikes even higher as the vampires continued to throw themselves at my shields. I sent out a blast of iridescent magic, flinging them away, hearing them impact stone, the crunch of bone. They would recover, but hopefully I bought myself enough time to focus on Sunny.

We must free her. My vampire showed me the image of Sebastian in the cavern, Sunny and Uncle Frank hovering over him while Dad and Theridialis watched. *You remember?*

Did I. We'd rescued Sebastian from her, my vampire, and Dad and Theridialis took her away.

To Demonicon. She shuddered. *A terrible place void of spirit, too far gone in blood magic and fire.*

I'm sorry, I sent as Sunny slashed at my shields. I felt her slice through, sealed the holes even as Uncle Frank joined her, a few of her vampires returning to fight. Gram looked grim, met my eyes.

I don't want to hurt her, she sent in a snarl. *Or my son. But I will if I have to.*

I know, I sent back. *We're working on it.* Knowing she

was probably eavesdropping anyway, I let Gram in on the conversation with my vampire. *Keep going*, I sent to her. *Demonicon.*

Your father contained me, she sent, still disgusted. *In that gem.*

Right. *Okay*, I sent as I shuddered from the pressure of Sunny's power. *What does that have to do with Sunny?* The queen dove headfirst for me, puncturing the outer layer of my shielding, pouring her darkened spirit magic into the surface of the wards. I felt myself weakening until my sorcery latched on and began to drain her. She shuddered and pulled away, howling to the ceiling, burning with white fire.

My vampire sighed as though I was dense. *You drew me out and contained me*, she sent.

Oh. Gotcha.

Gram prodded me. *Hurry the hell up*, she grumbled. *Before she hurts her damned self.* Sunny was now hurtling herself against the shields with abandon, gnawing on the edge as Uncle Frank pounded away with his spirit magic.

I need someone to channel it through. It had been Uncle Frank last time.

No, my vampire sent, *you don't. You have me.*

She was so smart I just wanted to smack her.

Bracing myself for the experience, fully open to my vampire, I let a small gap open in front of Sunny and stepped into it, reaching for her. She lunged at me, claws sinking into my arm, pain spiking, blood gushing from me, but it didn't matter.

I had her.

The taint came almost willingly, suctioned down into my sorcery, forming a writhing mass at my feet. I shuddered from it even as it raced through me, not hurting me, but stirring my nausea again. I wished there was some way to wash my insides and knew I'd be taking a very long and very hot shower at the first opportunity.

But I'd never be clean again.

Sunny gasped, her body returning to human form, claws retracting from my flesh as her eyes and mouth opened wide, blackness pouring from her and into me. Uncle Frank staggered, his darkness rushing to her and out again. I felt the oncoming rush of power before it appeared, the stain spread to Sunny's bloodline on every continent rushing back to source. I had just enough time to flinch before a great wave of taint burst against the stained glass window, shattering it inward, collapsing on Sunny and, in a surge of waste and rot, through me. The last of it burst from her, a bubble of filth, falling with a wet gurgle to meld with the rest.

Now, my vampire sent. *Contain it.*

She showed me an image, of the cavern in Wilding Springs where Sebastian had retreated to die. Flashed to me pulling her out of him, through Uncle Frank. To Dad. A shot of Demonicon, of her fighting my father, how he compressed her power, formed a gem from her very essence.

Gotcha.

I compressed the taint with my magic, corralling it into a single entity. It fought, writhing and struggling for freedom while my alter egos fenced it in. My sorcery spun beneath it, maji power crushing it with fire and my own blood still seeping from my arm, condensing it, tighter and tighter. It floated higher, rising to eye-level as it spun into facets, the size of a watermelon, a baseball, finally flashing on its edges as it imploded into a stone no bigger than a pea.

My vampire forced my hand out, opened my fingers, my palm itching with the need to pull away even as the gem spun on its axis before dropping into my waiting hand. The hard edges hummed with life, but I no longer felt the taint outside its confines, firmly trapped within.

I looked up and into Sunny's eyes as she stared at me in horror.

"Syd," she whispered. "What have I done?"

chapter twenty

I let the shield drop completely as the vampires around me either collapsed or stood stunned, looking around at each other, blinking, waking as though from a terrible dream. Uncle Frank came forward, hugged me, tall, strong body shaking.

"Love you," he whispered into my hair before turning to Gram and hugging her, too.

Sunny just stared at me with horror growing in her eyes, both hands clutching at her skirt, giant fistfuls of satin crushed under her grip. I stepped into her space, slid my arms around her and squeezed her, let her feel my love for her even as the gem with the taint pulsed softly in my fist.

She hugged me back, but it took some time, hands finally releasing their death grip on her skirt, rising to press against my back, cold cheek on mine.

"Thank you," she whispered.

"Sunny," I leaned back. "What happened?"

She shook her head, frown creasing her flawless face as she sank to the step behind her, head in her hands. "I don't know," she said. Uncle Frank joined her, the vampires of her court falling back, some whimpering, others crying softly as they held each other. Only Piotr glared at me still, though he embraced himself as though unwilling to look to others for comfort. "We returned after the wedding. And everything is fuzzy from there."

"Exactly," Uncle Frank said, one arm going around her shoulders. "I remember thinking how gray life seemed and then... nothing." He shook his head, blonde hair, grown almost to his shoulders, swinging. His blue eyes brimmed with anxiety. "So you tell us, Syd. What happened?"

"I'm sorry," I said. "This is my fault. I knew something was wrong, and you weren't talking to me, but I didn't come to find out why."

Sunny leaned against Uncle Frank. "Don't you dare apologize," she said. "I can tell by the look on your face you've had more things to worry about than us." She met her husband's eyes. "And we should have been able to take care of our own."

I wasn't the only one beating myself up, I guess.

"Enough stabbing yourselves with guilt," Gram snapped. Jabbed me in the ribs with one finger. "Tell them."

I did. Everything, knowing how little time I had, that dawn was coming. But they needed to know. From the wedding on. How Ameline tried to take over the Node on Demonicon, my adventures there, my trip to the Sidhe realm the first time around and almost losing Shaylee. Capturing Ameline. The loss of the Dumont magic thanks to the Brotherhood and subsequent return. And now, the Sidhe again, Sebastian's displacement. Ameline. And, the worst, Mom and her battle with the Council magic. I sank down to sit with them, feeling Sunny's fingers run through my hair, the comforting gesture I remembered from being a girl when they used to live with us, in cupboards in the basement. They, along with Sassafras, had been my constants when my life seemed so wrong.

How could I let them down like this?

"So you think the Brotherhood did this." Sunny let her fingers linger on my cheek. "To control us."

"And take your power eventually," I said. "I'm worried about Pannera."

Sunny nodded absently, eyes locked on the distance as a chill wind blew through the gaping hole in the back wall where the window used to be. She waved at it, off hand, a glowing white shield blocking the rising air current. "Considering their track record, I can only assume you're correct." She stood, taking my hand, pulling me to my feet, facing her people. "I've been compromised," she said, no nonsense, taking it all on herself. "And through me, all of you." They shuddered, exchanged worried looks. "And now, I fear, our sister clan, the Sthols, are also at risk." First time I heard the other clan in those terms. Was Sunny making headway to peace with Pannera before it all went to hell?

"My queen." Piotr's snarling voice cut through the fear and worry compressing the air in the room. "You've failed us."

The rest of the gathering gasped, but Sunny didn't hesitate. She flew past me, flashing around behind him. One hand gripped Piotr's throat, claws digging into his flesh as she hovered, teeth at his jugular.

"My queen," he choked, "what is your will?"

She let him go, shoved him so hard he fell, and though the others looked immediately more confident, I worried for her. Piotr's attitude wouldn't be stilled so easily.

I shouldn't have doubted her. Sunny's magic burst from her in a wash of white light, slicing through every vampire in the room, making them cry out in pain and fear.

"Go to your blood clans," she said, as cold and imperious as she had been when I first arrived. "Cleanse them if you must. Report back immediately. And Piotr." She turned to him. "Go to Castle Sthol. I would speak with Queen Pannera."

He gaped at her as though she just asked him to cut off his own leg. "My queen, dawn is coming." Gasped from between his lips, full of fear. I watched him wince, face crumbling under the pain of her order as he collapsed to his knees, clutching at his head. I knew that pain, felt it when Batsheva had control over me and a fraction of it earlier before I'd broken free of Sunny's command.

"Now," Sunny said, ever so softly.

With a cry of agony, Piotr, face a desperate mask, flickered into shadow and vanished.

I had no idea what Pannera would do to him if he wasn't welcome.

Frankly, didn't much care.

Besides, I was much too busy to worry about Piotr, especially when the air around me burst with blue magic and Margaret Applegate, surrounded by Enforcers, appeared in a flare of power.

Her glare told me I may have dodged one bullet, but she had me firmly in her sights for another barrage.

"Coven Leader Hayle," she said in her crisp British accent. "What are you doing in my territory?"

I didn't get to answer. Good thing, too. I probably would have been burned at the stake then and there for saying some rather rude things to a foreign Council Leader. Instead, Sunny pushed her way past me, glaring up at the floating witch.

"Council Leader Applegate," Sunny said, mimicking the woman's tone exactly, "what are *you* doing in *my* territory?

Best. Comeback. Ever.

Snort.

Margaret grumbled and Margaret glared but, under Sunny's furious cold gaze, Margaret finally relented. She pointed one finger at me, still bobbing in the air, ridiculously comfortable looking shoes swaying beneath her.

"This isn't over." And then, with a wave at her posse, the air flared blue again and she left.

I was in total crapola so deep I'd never shovel my way free when I got home. But I didn't care.

"Syd." Sunny turned me toward her. "We must talk to Miriam."

"Mom can't do anything." Uncle Frank looked so sad and so grim I wanted to hug him again. Okay, I wanted him to hug me and make me feel better. Wasn't going to happen. "We're on our own."

"The only way Pannera would allow Celeste to take over Sebastian's blood clan is if she was under the same influence we were." Sunny shook with the anger on her face. "We have to free her before something terrible happens."

"Why didn't the Brotherhood use us, since they had

us so deeply in thrall?" Uncle Frank's voice vibrated with emotion.

"I don't know," I said. "Unless they were holding you in some kind of reserve. Or you weren't completely under control yet."

True, my vampire sent. *If the taint had been allowed to progress further, we would never have been able to free the Wilhelms.*

"I know you're already in trouble," Sunny said, "but if you can free Pannera... Syd, we have to try."

This close to morning? Sunny was pushing it. I could feel the coming of dawn through my vampire, though she didn't keep me from moving around in daylight. But could we afford to wait?

No, Sunny was right. And I hated the idea of it. The Sthol Queen and I weren't exactly buddies. She'd claimed to want to help me when I was here last time, but I knew she'd throw me under the first bus to dead she could if it meant getting ahead.

And if someone who loved me could turn on me like Sunny did, what kind of reaction would I get from Pannera? Then again, it couldn't get much worse.

Could it?

I used the veil this time, despite Demetrius's offer to guide us. Instead, I let Sunny's memory guide me, taking her hand as she and I, Charlotte with us, stepped up to the slash in the barrier.

I turned to see Uncle Frank, one arm around Gram, nod to us as my grandmother hugged her son. Comical, the tall, handsome vampire and his scrawny, white-haired mother. But so much power surrounded the both of them, I wasn't worried.

"I'll be right back," I said.

Little did I know how prophetic my statement would turn out to be.

The gem of taint tucked into my front pocket for safe keeping, I stepped into the veil with Sunny and Charlotte.

Emerged on a windy mountain road at the gates of another castle, the night still deep, but softening in the east. To find a row of vampires waiting, scowling. And Margaret Applegate smiling grimly down on me from where she floated over head with her Enforcer bullies.

"Our queen does not wish to see you." I didn't know the vampire who spoke, a dark-haired young woman in appearance, though she stank of the taint now I knew what to feel for. "You are not welcome here."

Maybe if Margaret hadn't been there, we would have pushed the issue. She didn't give us the chance.

"That's it," she snapped. "You heard her. And, now that you're outside the realm of the Wilhelms and in my territory," she looked too satisfied for my liking, making me suspect the Brotherhood really did have a hold on her again, "I'm ordering you to leave." She hovered closer, lip curling into a sneer. "Not asking."

Fury did me no good. It just burned a hole inside me as I ripped open the veil again and retreated.

I hated losing.

CHAPTER TWENTY ONE

Margaret and her band of unmerry Enforcers appeared shortly after we returned to Castle Wilhelm. She barely gave me time to pick up Gram. Watching the Council Leader glare at me from outside the castle gates as Sunny led me inside, I considered staying, just to piss the woman off. After all, she had no authority in Sunny's domain.

But I'd stirred up enough trouble, from what I could tell, and I really didn't have time to play power games with a stubborn, old, British witch.

Sunny hugged me as we prepared to leave, sparing me a few more minutes despite the fact a line of vampires, growing by the second, clamored for her attention.

"I'll keep you updated on Pannera," she said, kissing me softly on the cheek. "I hate to lose the day, but I have no choice." Her eyes seemed haunted to me, though her face settled into her usual calm and kindness. I worried Sunny might punish herself too much for what happened and promised myself I'd be back as soon as I could to talk to her and offer what support I could.

When this was over.

If it ever ended.

"I'm coming with you." Uncle Frank had changed into jeans and a leather jacket, hair as short as I always remembered it. Not that a haircut and swap out of clothes could make him less attractive, but he looked more like his old self and less like a vampire. "Miriam might be fighting the Council's power but she—and it—can't ignore what's going on forever."

I silently wished him luck, sure he'd get about as far as I had, but welcoming the chance Mom might crack if her brother showed up.

Yeah, wasn't holding my breath.

Uncle Frank left us as we stepped out into the grass of the park into full night again, but not before hugging me. I was suddenly sixteen again, needing my tall, strong uncle to lean on, feeling his chilly body, unfed, leeching warmth from mine.

Syd, he sent. *I love you. Please, be careful.*

You too, I sent back. *Mom's... just be prepared, okay?* I let him see an image of her, as I'd seen her last and Uncle Frank flinched.

Damn her. He pulled away, looked down at me. *She's*

too stubborn for her own good.

Is that what you call it? I couldn't help the wry smile tugging at the corner of my mouth.

Uncle Frank laughed. "I guess it's my turn to see if I can make your mother cry."

That old joke actually made me giggle. "You can have that job," I said.

He reached for Gram, squeezed her until she swatted him. He planted a wet smack on her forehead.

"I'll need a place to crash." He winked at me. "Hope the basement is still available?"

"You bet." I waved, feeling a little forlorn, like he was riding off into a battle he'd never win as Uncle Frank saluted before flickering into shadow and disappearing.

I followed Gram and Charlotte into the yard, Demetrius hopping and bobbing beside me. When I finally met his eyes he pointed at my pocket.

"Kill it," he said.

Huh? My hand settled over the denim, the tiny bulge reminding me what I carried. I slipped the compressed taint out into the open air and had a look at it.

How innocent it seemed now, like a tiny black diamond, glittering in the light from over the back door.

"I take it you have a plan to destroy it?" I met Demetrius's gaze again and heard him groan in agony.

"You must," he said. Slammed both fists into his thighs several times before speaking again in a broken stutter. "But, d-d-don't let it o-o-out."

That would probably be bad. I let my power ease forward, felt around the edges of the gem, now nervous. "If it escapes, can I contain it again?"

My vampire answered this time. *There's no way of knowing*, she sent. *But if it does manage to flee, it could contaminate vampires here. Or worse, return to the Brotherhood.*

Why worse? They could have it as far as I was concerned.

My vampire's disgust with my attitude came through loud and clear. *There is a great deal of power contained in that gem*, she sent. Paused. *Almost as much as my own.*

Well, there was a revelation. *Are you saying this is some kind of alter you? Dark you?*

She shrugged inside me. *No*, she sent. *It has no sentience. But its power base has built in hundreds, if not thousands, of vampires.*

So destroying it won't be some walk in the park. Sigh. Nothing was easy, was it? I thought of the cave on the edge of my territory, the very one I'd only just shielded and hidden from view. *I think I know a place we can try it.*

Yes, she sent. *But not in the dark.*

Daylight, then. A few hours yet. I pocketed the gem and patted Demetrius's shoulder.

"I'll take care of it," I said with way more confidence than I felt. He sagged a little, shrugged and walked into the house like I'd disappointed him.

Wow. Sorry. I was only doing my best.

Not good enough vibes really weren't helping matters any.

I was barely inside the back door when I felt Liam's mind touch mine. Great. Probably more bad news. I braced myself, hanging on to the bottom post of the banister, hearing the others talking quietly in the kitchen as his power embraced me.

Thalion was here, he sent. *I couldn't reach you.* Could have come across as an accusation, but he managed to keep it gentle.

I was dealing with another problem, I sent, mental tone dry.

I assumed, he sent.

How are things in the realm? I sat on the bottom step, looking out the living room window into the street beyond, the lights casting cold illumination over the quiet block. I focused on that normal scene, took strength from it as he went on.

Not good, he sent. *He just wanted to update us. He spoke to Aoilainn who had him banished for speaking up.* Liam sighed. *She's totally deluding herself, Syd. The Unseelie are doing their best, holding off the deterioration, but I think there will come a point they just won't be able to any longer.*

Any idea how much time they have? I hugged myself, rocking a little, knees to my chest as I continued to stare. How could the world outside seem so normal when everything I knew was falling apart?

No, he sent. *But Thalion said he's starting to notice weakness on the Seelie side, so the queen's power to hide it has finally reached her limit.*

Though I knew Ameline was my only choice, I couldn't bring myself to act.

Coward? Maybe. But taking that step before I explored every possible angle was impossible. I just couldn't do it. Despite knowing I was out of options and had no other angle to run with.

Damn it, there had to be something.

I'm still working on it. I stood and turned, walking upstairs, going back to my room, body heavy with guilt and stress all over again.

Syd, Liam sent. *We can't let the Sidhe fall.*

Like I don't know that. I didn't mean to snap at him. But he took it gently.

Stay in touch, he sent before hugging me with his energy and letting me go.

To sag to the end of my bed in what felt like defeat.

No. I refused to be beaten. I lay back, closing my eyes, focusing on my power, calling out to the maji I was becoming.

And to her.

This time I am in control as I appear on the battlefield in the Enforcer realm. Iepa is waiting for me, a sad smile on her face.

Well done. *She lifts her hand to touch my cheek, but I slap her hand away.*

I'm not here for platitudes. I've had enough. We're out of time and options. I need to help the Sidhe now and I refuse to free Ameline until we try everything else.

Iepa nods. I warn you, they won't listen.

The other maji. We'll see about that.

My guide's shoulders round forward as her chin drops, but she nods again.

Wake.

I sat up, eyes wide, to find her standing next to me. I took me a moment to process this wasn't a dream.

Iepa was as beautiful in real life as she was in the sleeping world where we usually communicated, her golden hair shining in the low light I left on in the bathroom.

"Come then, Sydlynn," Iepa said, holding out one hand to me while the other gestured. The air parted, a slice opening in the veil. "Let us see if you are more persuasive than I."

chapTer Twenty Two

No rubbery membrane here, nor soap-bubble squeak. And no darkness devouring everything. Instead, when I stepped into the veil, a song welcomed me, a warm blanket and sunshine, a feeling of home like I'd never known before. When Demetrius had taken me to the vampire castle with his sorcery, I wanted to weep from terror and loss.

This time, the tears rose from joy.

We weren't in it long, the delicious place between my plane and the home of the maji. Just long enough I knew I would pine for the feeling for the rest of my life.

Until I found my own way back. And then I might never leave.

The feeling continued to a lesser extent as we exited the veil, the glowing seam sealing with a sigh of sound. I wiped at the wetness on my cheeks, unashamed as Iepa gently touched my hand.

"I know," she said in a voice vibrating with joy. "You are one of us, Sydlynn. This is what true power feels like."

I nodded, unable to speak just yet past the lump in my throat, instead taking a moment to absorb my surroundings.

The Sidhe realm was green, filled with beautiful landscapes and lush gardens, trees and streams of silvery water. I'd thought it beautiful, even without the Queen's glamour augmenting it. But she would whither in envy if she ever set foot on the maji plane.

"We call this Center," Iepa said, beginning to walk, her long, white skirt brushing with musical results over the grass. Grass so deeply green it almost glowed, each blade humming with life. I hated to walk on it, bending to slide my hands through the warmth, feeling the throbbing earth beneath, the call of creation magic flowing with generosity up into my fingers, climbing my arms, settling in my chest like a gift.

Iepa paused, smiled, waited without impatience as I wiped away another tear.

"This is amazing." I'd never seen a sky so brilliantly blue, almost like a crisp winter day when it took on that particularly amazing shade. This was even more intense, the air fresh and clean, warm on my skin. A soft, bouncing cloud hiccupped its way across the sky, more of a decoration than a threat of rain. I stumbled as my foot caught on the edge of a path when I finally moved forward, steadied by Iepa's gentle touch.

I gaped. Like an idiot. But didn't care even a little. Spread out before me was a shining city, all white marble and gold, greens and blues and reds swirling in vast mosaics of shining tile on walls and roofs. It reminded me of the images I'd seen of old Athens, ancient Greek architecture, but more, older, and defying the laws of gravity and physics.

"Center," Iepa repeated. "The home of all maji knowledge."

She got me moving again, each step carrying us rapidly closer until we were at the main gate. The Sidhe's particular way of traveling through their realm had come from the maji, obviously, vast distances covered in a few short steps. I looked up as we passed through the arching entry to the spiraling tower gracing the middle of the city, seemingly carved from stone and mist, frail and fragile while a hulking building, surely made for giants, spread out beneath it. Everywhere I looked was a new wonder, from the sparkling liquid of a waterfall pouring out of empty air and down over a rock wall to splash into a pool.

And, inside the pool, floating on what looked like giant leaves, were people.

Maji.

They ignored us, the three men and four women instead engaged in a heated discussion in languages I didn't recognize. One of the women spoke in high-pitched meeps while a man's voice rumbled, resembling the sound of crushing rock, not a language.

Iepa moved on, ignoring them, and I stayed with her, if only because her hand held mine.

A central fountain rose before us, buildings fanning out around it as we continued up the street. The stone turned from pale gray to more white marble, fusing with the giant fountain, the centerpiece a towering woman with her arms stretched up toward the sky.

"The first maji," Iepa said. "Aledora. The Creator made her first and from her all of us were made."

I shivered as we passed under her shadow, looking back over my shoulder at her as we left the fountain behind.

My mind swirled, stuttered, tried to comprehend, but it felt like a losing battle. I finally just allowed the feeling of Center to sweep me up, certain if I was permitted to come here, to live my life here, my immortality would be worth it.

The giant building loomed ahead, towering white spire climbing to the heavens above it.

"Center Hall," Iepa said, though now she sounded nervous. My hand clenched around hers in response. "Quickly, now."

She picked up her pace, drew me toward the monstrous steps. As she did, she grew beside me, taller, bigger until I understood, shaking myself free of some of my wonder in time to tap into my own ability. A simple trick, one my demon knew well, and soon I faced stairs of more normal proportion, though as I turned back to look at the rest of the city, I smiled at how tiny it now seemed.

"Sydlynn," Iepa's whisper caught my attention as we approached the gaping doors to the bright interior, "if anyone can convince them it will be you."

I wasn't so sure her confidence in me was well-founded, but we were about to find out.

The broad, open interior shone with sunlight, the roofless building wide open, a long shadow cast over the polished floors, a spiral of darkness from the tower above. I crushed my irrational fear the slender spike would crash down on top of us as Iepa led me to the middle of the room and a small circle of chairs.

Chairs filled with maji. At the far end was a larger chair, a little bulkier than the others. The occupant, along with all of the others gathered, looked up as we approached.

All of my anxiety fell away the moment he smiled at me, white beard close cropped, as sparkling as his teeth and pale gray eyes as he welcomed me with that smile.

"Iepa," he said in a deep, rich voice, laughter in it. "You've brought us a visitor?"

Iepa didn't seem impressed with his greeting, a frown

dipping her brows together. "Zeon," she said. "This is the one I spoke of. Sydlynn."

His smile didn't falter, nor did the others look at me unkindly. They all appeared old, though as vigorous as Iepa, and I wondered if they adopted their shining white hair and few wrinkles by choice.

"Ah, yes," he said. "Welcome to Center, my dear."

I bobbed a little curtsy before I thought about what I was doing, knowing it had to look ridiculous in my jeans and t-shirt. Zeon's belly laugh in answer made me grin. He stood, crossed the distance between us, white robe shining in the sun as he bent, at least a head taller than me, and took both of my hands in his.

The earth's vibration felt amazing, but the way Zeon's power zinged sent me into bliss. And, like this plane, he was generous with his power, sharing it with me even as I returned the favor.

It wasn't until I saw the flicker of a frown on his face I knew I'd done something wrong. But he didn't say anything to me, instead turning to Iepa.

"Oh, my dear," he said, shaking his head, still holding my hands. "What have you done?"

Um, what?

One of the women approached, pale gaze reminding me of Gram as she stroked one fingertip down my cheek. A tear welled in the corner of her eye before she shook her head and turned away. I glanced at Iepa, lost, not knowing what was going on, only to see her shoulders tighten, face locked in defiance.

"I did what fate dictated," she said, unrepentant, voice ringing through the room. A shadow passed over the sun and I glanced up, startled, to see a cloud bank move in. Zeon's face reflected the darkness above, but sadly, not in anger.

He turned back to me, grief as old as the Universe in his eyes. "You've come to ask for help," he said. "I'm sorry, but we can't give it."

My heart crushed in my chest as I gasped for a breath. "Why?"

He released me, sighed. "We don't interfere any longer." He turned and gestured at the others who rose and walked away, small groups forming, whispering to each other, but sad as Zeon when they met my eyes and departed. He ignored their exodus, led me to a chair, the clouds gathering further. The gloom overhead reminded me of the storm threatening the Sidhe realm. The image snapped me out of my adoration and into focus.

"We are merely shepherds," Zeon said. "Put here by the Creator to guide magical beings. But our task is long done." He glanced at Iepa who hadn't moved, still stared with her jaw clenched. "Worse, I'm afraid, we failed."

Well, they sure were failing now. "We need you," I said. "There is imbalance in our magic." I used the word specifically, knowing he wouldn't respond to anything else.

"There has always been," he said. "That is our failure. The Sidhe, they are beautiful and powerful, but empty of empathy." Zeon sat back in his chair, still mournful, like a grieving Santa Claus or amazing old grandfather I just wanted to hug. His power continued to radiate from him, without barriers, no shields or wards restraining him. My awe crept back without my permission as he went on. "The demons are also powerful, full of vigor and life. But the monsters inside them seek to devour their souls when they fully access that power." I had seen that first hand, felt it, in fact, both when I'd stripped my cousin Cypherion of his power and when Dad fought Vandelarius for Second Seat.

Not pretty.

He turned to my guide. "And the vampires, they are driven by their need for creation energy. Your attempt to become Creator has failed as well, my dear Iepa." He shook his head. "Your folly, thinking you could do what our Creator could not."

"At least I tried." I'd thought of Iepa as this all-powerful maji when we'd first met. And she never gave me reason to believe otherwise. But right now, in this moment, hearing Zeon chastise her, seeing her stand up to him, a surge of protectiveness and connection to her formed inside me.

She was me. Fighting for the right. Against a society

that wouldn't listen. Wouldn't see past their own failings.

My revelation was enough to shake loose the last of my private awe and stir my temper.

"What about witches?" Iepa's tiny smile told me I hit on a weak point in his argument.

Zeon's lips lifted without malice, fondness in his voice. "Yes, the witches," he said. "They showed the most promise. They lived, loved and created, no matter their short lifespans." His happiness faded. "But they, too, are afraid. Even now they hide from the truth, do they not?"

Damn it.

Zeon stood, offered me his hand. I took it, rose to face him as he bowed to me.

"I wish you well," he said. "But we will not interfere."

Chapter Twenty Three

My woken anger snapped like a cheap bra strap. "You blame the witches for being afraid, for not acting." I crossed my arms over my chest. "I'm kind of seeing some parallels here, if you know what I mean."

Another flash of a grin from Iepa. Okay then. I was really starting to like her.

Why hadn't I noticed before how much we were alike?

Zeon didn't react with anger, just more kindness, and I began to wonder if I could smother in it. The idea of living here, spending eternity here, wasn't as appealing as it had been. If a life of contemplation and inactivity waited for me in Center, I'd be making my home elsewhere, thanks.

"You made this mess." I shifted tactics. Let's see if guilt would help. "The sorcerers you created are trying to take over everything. And thanks to the way you made them, it's almost impossible for the other races to fight back."

Finally, a flicker of answering anger from him. It didn't last. Zeon clasped his hands in front of his belly and sighed. I was getting tired of his sighs. "There are those of our race who do not follow the path of natural evolution," he said. "They are at fault, not we."

Talk about passing the buck. "So because these dark maji didn't play nice, we have to suffer the consequences? While you stand around and moan and whine it wasn't your fault?" Wound up? Getting there. The once delicious feeling of Center now made my skin crawl, Zeon's openness with his magic turning my stomach in its arrogance. "We can't do this on our own. We need you to level the playing field."

Zeon didn't speak, his expression still calm and sad.

Ack.

I reached out to him with my power, let him feel me again. "I'm not asking you to do it alone," I said. "I'm perfectly capable of dealing with things on the ground. But the Sidhe are in trouble, and so are the vampires. Some backup, knowing I'm not alone out there, will mean the difference between success and failure."

He gently raised a shield between our power, the first I'd felt from him, cutting me off as easily as I'd done to others in the past. Weird to be on the other side of powerful magic for once and not be able to fight my way inside no matter how righteous the cause.

"You are not to be," he said. "No maji were ever meant to be born again." His blue eyes met Iepa's. "But now that you are, we will not unmake you."

Whoa. That was an option? I spun on Iepa who ignored me in favor of scowling at Zeon.

"The prophecy is clear." Her clenched fists bounced against her thighs in clear frustration.

"A prophecy only those of the dark heed." Zeon turned away, head down, hands behind his back before turning toward us again. He began to glow, rainbow power spiraling around him as he spoke. "If the magical races fall, so be it. We will be here to start anew. As is the Creator's will." He met my eyes as he began to fade, translucent, the chair behind him clearer and clearer through his form. "I wish you well," he said. "But you will fail."

And then, he was gone.

Oh *hell* no.

I spun on Iepa, pent-up fury needing to lash at her, but the frustration and answering anger on her face was enough to stop my assault.

She wasn't the enemy. From what I now knew, she wanted to help all along.

"What's to keep you from lending a hand directly?" I paced in front of the circle of chairs, shaking my hands to release some tension.

"I can't." Her words came out in a groan. "They won't let me." She trembled with her own emotions. "I've barely been able to come to you as it is."

"But the dark maji don't have that problem, do they?" I watched Iepa shake her head, golden hair whipping around her. "Will they help us?"

She gasped, stared at me like I slapped her. "We can't go to them."

"Why not?" I stomped off, tired of being there, wanting to go home. The appeal of the maji had worn off. "At least we could have backup. They want to defeat the Brotherhood, too, don't they?"

She grasped my arm, pulled me up short at the bottom of the stairs as both of us began to shrink.

"The only way to gain their assistance," she said, "is to free their daughter."

Ameline.

Why was I not surprised?

"We can't ask?" Yeah, bad idea. I knew it before the words left my mouth.

Iepa started walking, head down. "I already have," she whispered.

I stopped in the street, grabbed her, hugged her hard. For being so brave. I'd been mad at her for a long time, treated her badly because I didn't understand. But I understood now.

"It'll be okay," I said. "We'll figure it out."

Iepa hugged me back before leaning away and nodding.

"I know we will. Prophecy or not, Sydlynn Hayle, I have faith in you."

No pressure or anything.

Iepa parted the veil the moment we left the gates. I basked in the love and warmth of the trip, my room dark and uninviting as we stepped through again. I wrapped my arms around myself and turned to her, wishing I could follow Iepa back into the veil and stay there.

"There are two ways to fight the Brotherhood," Iepa said. "One, we go to war, all the races combined."

"But the races won't work together," I said. "That's been the problem all along. They barely get along with their own kind, let alone combining forces with different powers."

She nodded sadly.

"And the other?" I already knew the other.

"You and she," Iepa said. "Two maji, one dark, one light. Unstoppable."

So no war necessary.

"Why haven't the Brotherhood tried to take me out yet? If I'm such a threat. If Ameline is." Yes, they tried. But not very hard.

Iepa shrugged, suddenly desperate. "I don't know," she said, voice bordering on a musical wail. "I can only guess, in their arrogance, they would never believe two witches could truly become maji. Or that those emerging maji could unravel what they have created. Or that you would willingly allow Ameline to develop into her potential. But once you act, when you free her, they will know, Sydlynn." She touched my cheek, fingers vibrating with tension. "And they will come for both of you."

Good to know.

"Tell me what to do." Damn it, damn it. Was I really going to set Ameline loose?

"You must bring her to the chamber," Iepa said, backing into the veil. "Only there can we find balance."

I winced at the sour taste in my mouth.

Right, so free Ameline, putting my own life at risk, trigger an attack from the Brotherhood while sneaking into the vampire mansion where I'd been expressly told I wasn't welcome all to make sure Ameline had all the power of the dark maji.

Sounded like a great plan to me.

CHAPTER TWENTY FOUR

Iepa was already retreating, about to leave me, when I latched onto her with my maji power, anger returning. Sure, she'd proven she was on my side, okay. But I still had questions.

"You could have told me I was in imminent danger of being wiped out," I said.

She didn't fight me as I held her, hovering on the edge of the gash she'd made in the veil. "There was little reason to worry you. Either he and the others would destroy you, or they wouldn't. Prevention of the former was impossible."

Far too practical for my taste. "Any idea when the Brotherhood will be ready for an all-out assault? If I don't free Ameline?"

Iepa spread her hands in front of her, palms down. "No way of knowing," she said, "but I feel it is close.

Very close. If the Sidhe are allowed to fall, I have no doubt the Brotherhood will take that as the sign they need to act."

Yet another reason I had to save their arrogant Fey asses.

"Remember," Iepa said, "Ameline still needs time to develop into full power. You were delivered what you needed in full force. She must grow what she requires to match you."

Funny, I thought things always came easier for the bad guys.

Iepa finally pulled against me, gently, though, from the weight of her magic she could break free of me if she wanted to. "I must go," she said. "I will try to reason with the dark maji while you retrieve their daughter."

I let her leave without a fight, feeling the last of the warmth leave the room as the veil sealed behind her. Only the light from the bathroom illuminated the space, though, as I turned, I noticed the thin red line of dawn shining through my window. I retreated to the sink in my bathroom, splashing my face with water, staring at my tired expression in the mirror. The subtle hum of the taint gem buzzed against my hip, one hand falling to pat the pocket though I knew it was still there.

I really had to get rid of the damned thing.

It wasn't until I left my room, on my way to the stairs, I stopped with a start. Charlotte's door stood open a crack, but there was no sign of my bodywere. Not that she slept much. I knew she patrolled late at night. But she hadn't said boo about me leaving this time and, oddly, I started counting up the times she'd reacted badly to me going anywhere without her in the past month or so.

I shook my head and kept moving, promising myself I'd sit her down and talk to her once this present disaster was dealt with. And no amount of weregirl stoicism would keep me from finding out what was wrong.

Shenka sat in the kitchen over a cup of coffee, looking out the window with Sassafras curled up on his placemat next to her. She smiled and rose, came to hug me before pouring me my own cup as I sank with a sigh into my seat.

Magic topped up my cup with milk and sugar. The scent alone made me feel perky, the soft feel of Sassy's fur under my free hand helping, too.

They weren't going to like what I had to tell them, but I owed the pair of them the rest of the story. They both listened quietly until I fell silent, now moodier than ever, staring into the cooling coffee in my mug.

"You have to free Ameline." Shenka laughed without humor. "I can't believe I'm saying that, but you must."

"Agreed." Sassafras nudged my hand with his nose. "We're out of options and the Sidhe are running out of time."

Right on cue, Liam's mind reached for me. *Thalion's*

here.

The tension in his mental voice made me sit up straighter. *Trouble?* Dumb question.

You could say that, Liam sent, though with an edge of anger in his mind.

I stood, hugged Shenka again, kissed Sassafras and walked out into the early morning. Reached for the veil. Felt a hand take mine. I looked back over my shoulder into Charlotte's blank stare before pulling her along with me.

The steps to the basement of town hall were dark, Liam waiting for us at the bottom. Weird to be able to appear inside the building. There was a time when the Sidhe Gate kept me from riding the veil to anywhere near the interior, forcing me to use the lawn. Liam's eyes widened as I descended and hugged him, as concerned with the change as I was.

I followed him inside the cavern, feeling the wards at the entrance weaker than I remembered, sluggish to act. While I shivered over what that had to mean for the Sidhe, not for the first time, my mind went to Sonja O'Dane. Yes, I had bigger problems, like the imminent downfall of an entire race. And yet, I couldn't help but wonder where Liam's meddling mother had run off to, petulant thought vanishing as I joined Thalion in the Gate room.

"Sydlynn." It was the first time he'd called me by my

name. Shaylee sighed sadly and I realized then how much she would miss his devotion.

She could mourn later. "What's up?" Images of the Sidhe realm crumbling to dust, of the Brotherhood sweeping in and devouring everything, drove little spikes of feverish need into my flesh, making me antsy.

But Thalion's unhappy expression told me not only was I not going to like what he had to say, it had nothing to do with the Brotherhood.

"I've been geased," he said in a growling voice so unlike his normal velvet tone I flinched, "to escort you," bring me by force, in other words, "before Queen Aoilainn of the Seelie and explain why you are attacking our people."

Oh no, she did *not* just put this crap on me.

"With pleasure," I snarled.

And the pleasure would be all mine.

You betcha.

chapter twenty five

I didn't go with him right away. Nope, not yet. I had something to retrieve first.

Not that I expected my crystal to be able to help me much, but I was determined from here on in not to go anywhere without it.

I dug it out of my underwear drawer, flashing back to the stairs, Charlotte silent, along for the ride, before striding into the cavern and straight through the already open gate, not waiting for Thalion to lead the way.

She'd put a geas on one of her own Sidhe to force me to face her. Well now. We'd just see about that, wouldn't we? And her little plan to blame all of this on me?

She didn't get to point fingers.

I covered the ground in massive strides, maintaining my natural form, again with Shaylee's full support. From the way the earth vibrated under me, how the very grass and trees seemed to shrink from my stomping feet, I knew I was making the kind of entrance I'd hoped for.

By the time I stormed over the fancy little bridge and into the main clearing, I gathered a big enough head of steam a strong gust of wind actually pushed before me, blowing over the gathered court, flapping skirts and ruffling perfect updos, sending the gauzy white fabric over the queen's pavilion into a frenzy of snapping.

She glared and I glared right back, coming to a halt before her, arms crossed over my chest. I'd taken a lot of crap in my day, but no way was some spoiled, stubborn, arrogant Sidhe going to push me around when I was trying to save her pathetic butt.

No. Way.

The queen's fury rolled over me like an earthquake, but I held my ground, creation magic slicing it open, sorcery siphoning off the excess. Aoilainn looked as beautiful as ever, but the faintest tint of decay had begun here, too, around the edges of the pavilion. Was the grass not quite so lovely, her dress perhaps slightly wrinkled? And her skin, normally poreless and translucent, seemed common, marked with the beginning of wrinkles and minute flaws that made her appear more human.

"It is you!" She pointed a shaking finger at me. "I feel your foul darkness devouring my magic. You have brought this pestilence upon us!"

Enough. Just freaking enough already. I gathered up

my maji power and firmly shoved her back into her throne, pinning her there while I fought my temper.

"Listen up," I snarled while Charlotte's wolf form snapped in counterpoint. "I've tried to warn you in the past, but you just won't hear me. Guess what? I'm not giving you a choice this time."

Her whole court stared, some with fury, others in fear. But Thalion held his ground next to me, so they didn't move. For now. I wondered how long that would last, when the first of the queen's soldiers would finally act.

I just hoped I wouldn't have to kill any of them.

Aoilainn's face blanched even whiter than usual. "It must be you," she whispered.

"They are called the Brotherhood." I know I probably shouldn't have spoken to her so slowly, like she was a child without a clue, but it was hard not to use sarcasm. It was either that or shake her so hard her head popped off.

Shaylee might not have liked her mother very much anymore, but I didn't think she'd appreciate me decapitating her.

Aoilainn shuddered, one hand covering her mouth. Eyes full of desperate terror, her fury turning to fear so fast I did a double take, the queen sobbed once as a large patch of decay appeared in response to her loss of control. Several of the court Sidhe screamed and fainted, not all of them women, while the Queen pulled herself back together.

"You must help us." She reached for me. "My daughter, I beg you."

Shaylee shuddered and turned away while I let my vampire and demon comfort her at the sight of her mother fallen so low.

"I offered once before," I said. "You kicked me out of your kingdom, if you recall. And I told you I wouldn't care if you fell. Do you remember?"

Aoilainn nodded, mute. She sank back into her throne. It was only then I noticed she sat alone, her prince consort nowhere to be seen. Coward was probably hiding in his room hoping this all went away.

Anger bubbled inside me, triggered by my frustration and the knowledge I had to take steps that would put not only me but my whole family in danger. All for this ungrateful, spoiled queen. It was almost too much. I wanted to walk away.

Please, Thalion reached for me. *Don't punish all of us for the actions of one.*

He sent me an image of the Unseelie and I sighed, temper fading, leaving a ball of burning yuck in my stomach.

I met Aoilainn's eyes as she straightened, her queenness returning.

"You're not going to like it," I said. "But you need to work with King Odhran if you want this to stop." Okay, that was a lie. I felt Thalion twitch next to me as Shaylee gasped, but chuckled.

Sneaky, she sent.

Aoilainn turned away, mouth grim. "Never," she said.

"Okay," I said, turning away. "Have a great end of the Sidhe. Let me know how it turns out."

I made it two very determined strides before her magic reached me, along with her voice.

"You can't leave me!"

I turned back and gave her a view of my extended middle finger.

"Like hell," I said. And walked away.

Thalion was silent the rest of the way to the border, though he seemed to be free of the Queen's geas at least. When we came to the gate between Seelie and Unseelie territory, he sighed like he'd lost his true love.

Which, I guess, he had.

"I fear we will not survive if the realm is allowed to fall," he said. "Prepare yourself."

Not good. I stepped over the border and into hell.

Unseelie lay, collapsed and fading, scattered across the dead grass. Large lumps like old stones made hillocks of rock in a semi-circle around two thrones made of twigs and branches. I caught my breath as I realize those hills were the Unseelie giants I'd met my first time here, kind and gentle, sweet natured. Far more than any Seelie I'd met, no matter how they compared on the outside. The power drain had forced them to the earth, their large eyes closed, bodies rigid. And they weren't alone.

The thrones held the sagging forms of the king and queen, both of whom didn't attempt to rise as I approached. A large, black blot, reminiscent of the passage Demetrius used to take me to Wilhelm Castle loomed above, the heart of the storm eating the sky.

"I take it you have no further help to offer." Odhran grunted as he forced himself to sit up, face lined with weariness.

Agony burst from the ball of bubbling grossness in my stomach, fed by overwhelming frustration.

Instead of answering him, I turned and looked up. Lifted my crystal in my hand and focused on the gaping nothingness. My sorcery answered immediately, eagerly, no longer hungry, but starving. And, for a brief moment, I thought I had the key.

Ravenous and powerful, the black flower unfolded, channeled through the living crystal, and began to reverse the process. I felt the sudden rush of Sidhe power, flowing back through the nothingness and into me, my crystal pulsing green. A gust of wind flattened my clothing against me as the force of my sorcery, sucked at the disappearing magic, a sigh of power echoing over the fading Sidhe.

But, within moments I no longer drew power, only defended it. Felt it begin to trickle away from me again. With a snarl of rage I gathered what I had left and tied it to my creation magic, making the edges sticky with air magic tied to the earth, before slamming it into place over the hole.

The patch suctioned to the edges of the nothingness, flattening out, warbling as it hummed with tension. I held my breath for a long moment, staring, watching as the Unseelie sighed and straightened, looking up with me.

The patch groaned, hummed, vibrated.

Held.

Holy. Okay then.

I spun on Odhran with a grim expression, crystal held in my hand so tightly I was sure I'd see blood flow out from between my fingers any second now. He reached out to squeeze my shoulder with a small smile, already regaining strength.

"Well done," he said.

"I have no idea how long it will last." I glanced up, watched my sparkling, iridescent patch waver. "But if you can feed it power, it should keep the siphoning from continuing until I can get back."

"You have a plan then." He looked up, hands forming fists.

I sighed and nodded, chest tight, wanting to throw up.

"I do," I said. "I have to go break someone out of prison."

CHAPTER TWENTY SIX

Varity's mind felt startled when I reached for her, but she quickly sobered when I told her what I needed.

I'll meet you at the chapel, she sent. *You're coming alone, I take it?*

I couldn't bring Gram. No way was I involving her in the jailbreak when it could mean more trouble for our family later. *Just Charlotte and I*, I sent.

She had robes in her arms when we arrived, offered me mine without comment, but hugged me when I'd finished draping myself.

"She's so proud of you." Varity's eyes glistened with tears, lower lip trembling a little. "You're Ethie's granddaughter all right." Lips curving into a ferocious grin, she tore open the veil to the stronghold, the pull of her Enforcer magic skimming around the edges. "Just promise me you'll let me in on the action when you strip this wretched girl dry."

Oh, did I forget to tell her I planned to break Ameline out? That I'd lied to her, explaining I just needed to "see" the prisoner, wink wink, nudge nudge?

I was going to hell and never, ever getting out.

Yes, it sucked lying to Gram's friend, lying to Gram, too, for that matter. But I had to protect them both if I could and there was no way she'd let me just mosey on out of the Enforcer plane with Witches Most Wanted in my company.

I used to suck at lying. Probably should have bothered me I was clearly getting better at it.

Worries for another time.

Varity's power felt different from Gram's, though it had the same Enforcer weight. I followed her as I had my grandmother, Charlotte again taking up the last position, my head down and tension mounting. This time I wasn't just going for information. Part of me couldn't believe I was actually here, in the stronghold, on my way to betray witches everywhere. The Council. My mother.

My principles.

What good was any of that, if the world ended because I didn't act?

Way to excuse questionable behavior, Hayle. Just keep telling yourself you don't have a choice.

Sigh.

The climb up the tower stairs burned as much this

time as it did the last, though my steady workouts with Sage added to my endurance so I wasn't a total loss by the time Varity paused outside the door. I waited for her to lead the way and entered the circular hallway, reaching the same stretch of corridor we had last time. She thralled the watching Enforcers without a moment's hesitation and I wondered if she and Gram had done something like this before.

Wouldn't surprise me at all.

"I'll be right back." I paused and hugged her quickly, my heart pounding for what I was about to do.

More accurately, for what Charlotte was about to do. As I pulled away, my wereguard lashed out with one fist, taking the old Enforcer in the temple. I almost cried out, not expecting the blow, watching as Varity's eyes rolled up in her head and she tumbled to the ground without a sound. I spun, staring at the Enforcer guards she'd thralled, terrified they'd wake and see us only to catch their slow-motion collapse. Varity's power must have taken them out when she was knocked unconscious.

Lucky. Damned freaking lucky. I turned to snarl at Charlotte who stared grimly back.

"We don't have time," she said. "Get her and let's go."

Damn it. How were we going to escape without Varity?

I turned, a long and furious lecture for Charlotte in the works while I stomped to the door, only to have my vampire whisper as I reached for the handle of the cell entry.

You can open the way, she sent. *You are maji.*

Um. Oh. Yeah.

Duh, Syd.

I jerked the door wide to find Ameline standing, hands folded before her. Smiling. Waiting for me.

"Finally," she said, striding forward, brushing past me, going right to Varity. "I thought you'd never get here." I stared at her, body shaking with anxiety as she rudely stripped the old Enforcer of her robe and donned it over her thin, white robe, dark hair swept under the black hood. Ice blue eyes met mine, bow mouth forming a little smile.

So. Much. Hate. I wanted to kill Ameline myself, tear her apart with my bare hands. Not follow her as she turned and strode off, Charlotte growling under her breath. What the hell was I thinking? I should be pinning her ass to the ground and cutting off her power, not trailing after her down the circle of stairs to ground level, staring at the floor as we hurried back the way we came. How Ameline knew where to go I had no idea, but she led and I followed, my chest knocking heavily with the pounding of my heart and breath catching in little hitching gasps as I fought the urge to throttle her.

We made it to the exit passage without incident, Ameline tossing back her hood as she turned to me and gestured at the stone wall.

"If you would." Like I was her servant. I pushed past her, harsher than necessary, reaching for the veil between the Enforcer plane and mine.

For a moment, I couldn't find it and I actually felt better. Okay then, this wasn't going to work. Back to Ameline's cell it was and I'd somehow explain things to Varity. But just as I was about to quit, happily, relieved even, I felt the connection to home wake and the veil opened before me.

Ameline tried to march past me, but I held her back with one hand. One shaking hand. "If you screw with me, I will kill you."

She still had that damned smile on her face. "We have a common goal," she said, the "for now" unspoken, hanging between us. "And we both have a job to do. If you want the Sidhe to survive, I suggest we get to it."

How the bloody hell did she know about the Sidhe? Didn't matter now. Not while we stepped over the line, into my plane, onto the grass outside the chapel in Harvard Yard.

Up until this point, I'd broken laws, yes. But this, passing into my world with Ameline beside me, this was so real I almost choked on it.

A firm grip on her arm stopped her before she made it very far.

"We have our orders," I snarled. "And I'm following

them to the letter."

She jerked herself free, lips curling before she shrugged. "I'm eager to see this maji chamber of yours," she said with a satisfied smirk. Like she knew I was in the dark, had no idea where her information came from.

Hated her even more for it.

The veil protested her presence, Ahbi's spirit fighting me as I tried to ride to the vampire mansion. Not like I blamed her. Ameline murdered her, left her bleeding on the floor for me to find, tricked my grandmother into thinking she was me. But I'd done what I'd done and I couldn't let her stop me out of some sense of vengeance she ultimately couldn't do anything about.

I finally had to cut my grandmother off, separating my demon from Ahbi's spirit touch before she sulkily gave in and let us go.

Ameline stepped out of the veil like Ahbi hadn't almost eaten her whole and never released her again, icy gaze locked on the mansion. At least it was daylight still. I wouldn't have Celeste to worry about. But if Stewart gave me a hard time, I didn't think I had it in me to hurt him.

One glance at Charlotte told me I wouldn't have to. She'd do my dirty work for me as often as she could. And while I hated the thought of her being a bully, she did come in rather handy, at that.

"Why did you drop us here?" Ameline's condescension was going to grow very old, very fast.

"Because," I said through clenched teeth as I stormed past her, "this is as far as we can go on the veil. What's the matter, Ameline? Forgot how to walk?"

I didn't bother to turn around and see if she frowned in reply, leaving it up to Charlotte to herd the other witch toward the mansion. My power kept a careful watch on her, though. No way was I letting her dodge off when I really did need her.

Damn it.

And no way was I telling her I tried to take us directly below. Or that despite my vampire's presence, the blood clan's wards rejected me. That her presence upset my demon grandmother's spirit so much I couldn't focus my maji power. Because if I did, I probably would have ended up screaming at her for about an hour and we were running low on time. And daylight.

I didn't bother to knock. Stewart or no Stewart, I had to reach the chamber and being all nice about things when nice had gone out the window wasn't going to cut it. He emerged from a side door at a run while the echoing boom of the door crashing open still reverberated through the giant foyer, skidding to a halt on the polished stone floor as I stomped my way past him. Stewart's face flickered between relief and fear as he followed me, keeping pace.

"You have an hour at the best," he said in a low voice, as though the vampires could hear him. "When she rises,

I'll have no choice."

"Did she order you to keep me out?" I spun toward the door at the end of the hall, slammed it open on my way to the secret passage below.

"She did," he said, jaw clenched and face flushed. "But you are always welcome here."

I turned to Stewart, felt his pain. Not as powerful as the agony I experienced, but pretty weighty for a normal. "I'm sorry," I said, really meaning it. "I didn't want you to be hurt."

"My true master lies locked in his coffin," he said, voice gruff. "The very least I can endure is a little pain if it means his freedom." Hope crossed his face. "Please, tell me you will free my lord?"

I so did not have time for this. "I promise," I said, as Charlotte tapped the stones on the wall, Ameline watching with her judging blue eyes, "when this mess is handled, I'll come for Sebastian."

Stewart's grimace held thanks. "I knew you would," he said. "Now hurry and do what you must."

I left him there, an old worry now fresh on my mind, as stone ground together. One hand firmly gripping Ameline's Enforcer robe, I descended the stairs appearing beneath me, dragging Ameline behind me.

chapter twenty seven

The moment we reached the bottom, I propelled Ameline ahead of me. She stumbled, spun to snarl, only to find Charlotte in her face, her wolf emerging just enough her snout pressed a wet mark into Ameline's cheek.

I grinned, all anger, no humor. "Try it," I said. "I'd love to see what a mess Charlotte's teeth will make of your throat."

Ameline shoved my bodywere aside. "You need me." She pointed one long, slender finger at me. "Don't forget it." Spun and marched off, the queen of absolutely nothing.

I squeezed Charlotte's shoulder as we went after her. "Nice," I said. "But I really do, I guess."

Charlotte bared her teeth at me, her wolf in her eyes. "I can hurt her so much she'll never recover and still leave her breathing."

Good to know.

Ameline entered the second chamber, going right to the staircase. I'd never figured out how to close it and so it remained, waiting for us. Rough stone carved with names and history passed under my fingertips as we descended, the past meeting the present as we finally reached the bottom and passed over the threshold into the main chamber.

Ameline went immediately to the stone platform in the center of the room and hopped up on it, crossing her legs and her arms over her chest, looking down on me from her self-made throne. She really was full of herself.

This had to be over, now. I slapped one hand down on the stone and reached for Iepa.

Felt her answer immediately.

Knew just as quickly she wasn't alone.

I hated how I gaped for a second as Iepa appeared, a handsome man standing next to her. Where my maji guide was dressed in a white robe, golden hair worn over her shoulders like a cloak, his skin was dark, the color of burned toast, eyes a pale amber two shades lighter than my demon's. He smiled at me before turning to Ameline, deep crimson robe almost black as it swung with his movement.

"At last," he said.

Ameline stayed where she was, meeting his eyes like

an equal.

"Your information was most helpful," she said in her clear, emotionless voice.

The source of her intel.

Her own maji guide.

Iepa met my gaze, shook her head a little, her power touching mine as my temper rose and crested, at the breaking point. Would have been nice to know we both had guides.

Sydlynn, my vampire sent. *You honestly didn't think of it?*

Grumble, mumble.

"The time is nigh." The dark maji turned to Iepa.

"We have fulfilled the conditions of the prophecy." She held out her hand to him and he took it, magic passing between them. I expected his to be black or blood red, but it was the same shining iridescence I'd come to expect from Iepa. No fair the bad guys got to have our sparkly power.

No fair.

"How nice," I said, words edged and furious. "So happy to be of service. But the Sidhe are in a bit of trouble, in case you two weren't aware, and we are almost out of time."

"Agreed." The dark maji bowed his head to me. "I am Trinol, Sydlynn."

Whatever.

"Good for you," I said. Focused on Iepa who sighed

at me. "Well? I broke her ass out of prison because everyone's been telling me we need balance or some other such magic mumbo jumbo. I've put my whole family in danger and my own neck on the chopping block. Can we please actually do some freaking good already?"

"How delightful." Trinol's lips twitched before he bowed his head to me again. "Perhaps I've been assigned to the wrong maji."

Ameline's eyes tightened as she tapped one foot on the floor, bare toes pattering against the stone. "How do we save the Sidhe?"

"You must work in tandem," Iepa said. "Go to the Sidhe realm and use your bonded magic to sever the control the Brotherhood has over their kingdoms, releasing the combined Fey magic from its prison."

She said what?

Even Ameline looked a little ill. "Bonded?"

"That is why it was necessary to bring you here." Iepa crossed to one of the sections on the wall. There I saw names I knew, from my ancestor Auburdeen, through her children, grandchildren and finally to Gram, Mom, Uncle Frank, Meira and me. Iepa pointed to us before Trinol turned and crossed to the other side of the room. Both Ameline and I spun together to watch him, me with a terrible knot of worry in my chest, Ameline with pursed lips.

When he pointed out her name, a list of others

behind her, Ameline hissed before spinning on me.

"Well now, cousin dear," she said. "It would appear Grandfather Ivan gave you more than Dumont good looks."

My cousin?

If I could have bathed my brain in acid to erase what I'd just learned, I would have happily done so. Couldn't. Was forced to stand there and absorb the truth.

We were related.

"Far more closely related than even Ameline knew," Iepa whispered in my ear. I shivered, hadn't noticed she crossed to my side as Trinol watched me with his pale yellow eyes. "Your grandfather and Odette Dumont had a child. One Ivan forced her to give up for fear Ethpeal would discover his betrayal. And because such a child would be forbidden."

Gram. What would knowing Ivan betrayed her do to Gram?

"My mother." Ameline's shoulders twitched. "Heir to the Dumont family by blood, not just by training."

The satisfaction in her voice made me want to slap her. But so many things slid into place at that point. How Odette nurtured and protected Ameline, grooming her to take over the family coven despite the fact she wasn't a Dumont. Because she knew all along she'd be handing over power to her own granddaughter.

"How screwed up is that?" I turned to Ameline,

smiled sweetly even as my heart crumbled for Gram who had already lost so much. "Your dear, darling grandmother tossed you over for your weak cousin Mia so she wouldn't have to give up the secret of your birth."

There had been a handful of times Ameline really showed emotion. But this was the first instance I saw her stripped to her core, pure hate and rage burning deep inside her, devouring her soul even as she slammed up her defenses again and spun away from me.

Oh snap.

My vampire stirred, perking up. *Darkness comes*, she sent.

"We're out of time." I shuddered as I turned to Iepa. "What do we have to do?"

It was Trinol who came to me, to Ameline, and took our hands in his. Forced us to touch. "The Dark and the Light must come together as one," he said, voice droning as though repeating something he'd memorized. "One spirit, one power, two minds, two bodies. And when the empty ones rise, only the bonded will have the unity to create what is being destroyed."

Yada yada, dude. "Just hurry up," I snarled. "The sun's coming up."

Anger glinted in his gaze, dark face tightening. "The task is yours," he said. "We have only brought you together."

That was so freaking not helpful I wanted to scream.

I turned to Ameline, felt her resisting even as I did. My free hand slid into my pocket, brushing over the tainted gem before locking around my crystal, the touch of it waking the dark flower beneath me. My maji energy came forward easily, the power of the cavern making it simple to call. But even it rejected her, a thin, angry line of sizzling sparks forming between our palms, cascading to the floor and making me hiss from the heat.

"Together," Iepa said, leaning over my shoulder. "As one."

"Unless you're going to actually show me what that looks like," I said between clenched teeth as blisters burst open on my palm, still pressed firmly to Ameline's, "shut up."

I could hear Charlotte chuffing, turned to snarling, then a deep, warning growl, but didn't have the focus to pay attention to her. Not while Ameline's pale blue eyes burned through me, her own magic fighting as much as mine did.

Sydlynn, my vampire sent, *they know we're here*.

Out of time.

Teeth gritted, soul begging me to stop, I did the right thing, acted when she would not and opened my power to Ameline.

Let her in.

chapter twenty eight

Had anything ever felt so wrong and yet as though it was meant to be? My entire body burned with the joining of my power to Ameline's as her darkness raced around my edges, my light setting her on fire.

I felt the vampires appear, but only peripherally. Knew Iepa and Trinol had gone. Didn't matter we were alone because we weren't alone, Ameline and I.

We had each other and the multiple souls we carried. My vampire hissed at her budding undead spirit, my demon snarling at her young fire. Even Shaylee hummed unhappily at the small child who was the Sidhe within my nemesis. But our reactions to each other didn't matter. Not while the maji power, dark and light, combined and bonded us together.

It wasn't until I felt Charlotte's distress I pulled free of my hold on Ameline and turned to find Celeste and her vampires had us cornered. Thought they did, at least. And Charlotte stood with her back to me, bent in half, her wolf emerging, clothing torn in places from her shift as she snapped and swiped at the wary vampires.

I met Celeste's eyes, felt her fury turn to fear, set my hand on Charlotte's shoulder. "I'll be back for Sebastian," I said before tearing open the veil and pulling my bodywere after me.

And Ameline.

Always Ameline, from now on.

I could still feel her inside me. The connection felt similar to the one I shared with Gram, how we remained a part of each other through the family magic and the bond left behind by her power, magic I carried with me since infancy. But this was different, and as much as I loved Gram, more fundamental. Raw, down to the bone, settling into my cells, the core of my spirit, until there was nothing we didn't share.

Creeped me the hell out. But I had no options, and as much as I fought it on an intellectual level, my maji power welcomed her with open arms.

And her mine. Not only was she in me, I was in her. Felt the stirring of her heart past her icy shell. Didn't want to think of her as having a heart, for that matter. But she did. And it now beat in time with mine.

As we stepped out of the veil, I felt a moment of concern. I'd been aiming for Liam, as I always did, using him for my target when it came to traveling to the Sidhe Gate cavern. But instead of emerging in the side yard of town hall or even at the top of the stairs, I found myself stepping out onto the stone floor of the cavern itself this time, stopping only a few feet from the very startled Gatekeeper.

"The Sidhe?" Had they fallen? Was I too late? But no, the look on Liam's face told me he was more bemused than worried.

"No change, from what I can tell," he said. Looked down the hall to the entry and back to me again. "How?"

I shrugged, pretty sure I had an answer, but didn't get to give it. Not while Liam gasped and took a step forward, hands fisted, Galleytrot rushing forward with a low growl, black fur standing on end.

Oops. I stepped in front of Ameline as the pair finally noticed and then threatened her, hating I needed her even as our bond strengthened by the moment. "Ease up, guys," I said. "She's here to help."

Did I really just say that? Did those words really pass my lips?

"I'll believe that when it happens." Liam did back down, though Galleytrot didn't sit, fur trembling on end, eyes blazing red fire. Considering she'd almost killed him the last time they met, I hardly blamed him.

For that matter, she tried to kill most of the people I cared about.

Why was I working with her again?

Ameline ignored Liam's threatening stare and Galleytrot's rumbling growl shaking the ground under our feet. She brushed past me, past Charlotte, eyes locked on the Gate.

"This is a delightful reunion," she said, "but we really have work to do."

Liam's jaw jumped. I would have loved to see what he planned to do to her, I really would. But one touch of my hand made him settle, the Sidhe's plight more important than personal vendettas. His hazel eyes sparked with green magic as he looked down at me.

You can't be serious. His hands trembled as he brushed his fingers over my cheek. *Syd—*

I cut him off before he could give me a lecture. *If you can think of another way to save the Sidhe, I'm all ears.* I glared at Ameline's back. *Until then, it's her or nothing.*

Liam nodded after releasing a gust of air from his pursed lips. "Fine," he said, pressing a kiss to my forehead quickly before spinning and striding to the Gate. Green fire crackled around the edges as he pushed his power into it a little more aggressively than necessary. "I just hope this is worth it."

No kidding.

Ameline's smiled, condescending and freezing cold. "Just do as you're told, Gatekeeper," she said. "And leave the rest to us."

Wow, she was really asking for it.

I think Liam would have gladly opened the Gate just to be rid of her at that point. I just wished I had a way to cut myself loose, too. No such luck. But even as I wiggled and wriggled against contact, the longer we remained linked, the more powerful I felt.

Okay then. If I had to work with her, I could accept that. But if this connection tried to make me like her, I was out of here.

The moment we passed through the soap-bubble edge and into Sidhe territory, Ameline's tall, dark-haired form shrank, a little girl with pale green eyes and long brown hair replacing her. I stared down at her, forcing myself to swallow the lump of disgust rising in my throat at the sight.

Not Shaylee. She looked nothing like my Sidhe princess. And though I'd been sure Ameline hadn't used my alter ego to create this young Sidhe soul when she held her in thrall, I still worried, just a little bit.

Not an infant. Mom told me she'd used two Sidhe souls to create a baby spirit. Looking down on her, an actually little Sidhe girl, I had a thought. Bronagh's daughter, and Cian's. The Queen's adviser and the force behind the Gates.

And, in a weird, gross way, Liam's.

I could not go there. Not. My brain would not process that in any possible hell Ameline's Sidhe soul was

Liam's child.

Oh. My. Swearword.

I couldn't think that way, had to tear my eyes from her flat stare, turn and force myself to march toward the border. Charlotte flanked Ameline's young form, loping along as the blonde wolf while Ameline's little body had no trouble keeping up with me. I was so focused on not looking at her, on just getting to the Unseelie side and dealing with the Brotherhood, I missed the fact we weren't alone.

Ameline's huff of irritation joined Charlotte's soft chuff of warning as I looked up.

And found myself surrounded by shining, golden Seelie soldiers.

Seriously? Annoyance bloomed as a large white horse emerged from the circle, Aoilainn mounted on its back. She'd traded her flowing gown for golden armor of her own, long hair caught up in an elaborate braid draped across her shoulders like a cloak. She glared down at me as the great horse pawed the ground beneath him.

But Aoilainn's attention didn't stay on me long, and while I gathered what was left of my temper and tried to put together a civil response to being ambushed like this, the queen's eyes settled on Ameline.

Her face flashed to rage so fast I almost missed it when she flung her arm forward, a ball of green fire arching toward the Sidhe girl form beside me. I reached out to block it the exact moment my co-maji did, the sphere bursting in a cascade of rainbow sparks.

"Arrest her!" Aoilainn's face contorted, tears standing in her eyes. "Thief and murderer, you've stolen the child of our most beloved Bronagh!"

Ameline smirked. Bad choice, as far as I was concerned, but she didn't seem to care.

"Come and try it," she said.

Aoilainn did, though her soldiers held back, her power pounding against us. I could feel the weakness of it, though, caught the decay in the air around us, in Aoilainn's armor, flashes of the dead grass painted green by her glamour as she did her best to destroy Ameline. I stood next to the witch turned little Sidhe girl, felt her gloat as Aoilainn's power failed, hated that Ameline enjoyed the queen's downfall so much.

And that I wasn't any better than Ameline when it came right down to it.

I finally put an end to the cascade of power, cutting Aoilainn off. The queen sagged in her saddle, weeping openly as I supported her with creation magic. She stared at me, mute and desperate as the sky overhead darkened and the grasses finally flickered to brown as her glamour failed. The girl next to me shifted to Ameline's form before settling into a child again.

The soul called to the realm. Either that or Ameline chose to remain as she was. Interesting choice.

Charlotte, in human form again, stood just behind me, eyes locked on the weeping queen.

"We are doomed," Aoilainn said.

"You're not," I said. "We can fix this. But only if you do what we tell you."

She shuddered, but nodded. "I will," she said.

Would wonders never cease. Mighty Aoilainn had crumbled. Shaylee took no joy in it, but I had to admit I wasn't really all that empathetic. "We have to go to the border," I said. "And talk to Odhran."

Aoilainn's hesitation had to be instinctual. Old habit or born into her. Whatever the case, she visibly struggled with her answer before she bowed her head and sighed.

"Our people will die if I don't act," she said, humility radiating from her, probably for the first time in her entire existence. "I will do whatever is necessary."

I would probably have enjoyed the moment of triumph more if it hadn't been for the nasty grin on Ameline's little girl face.

ChApTeR TWeNTY NINe

We reached the border in moments, once Aoilainn ordered her people to stand aside. She looked so tired and worn I wondered if she put the last of her energy into moving us as quickly as possible. It seemed the air shimmered from a blank horizon to suddenly flaring with green flame and a gathered army of fading Unseelie.

I approached the doorway to the other side with Ameline next to me, gesturing for Odhran and Niamh to join us at the barrier. They came, looking as beaten down as Aoilainn, their people as weary. At least the giants sat up now, large eyes blinking slowly, sleepily, no longer prone and helpless. I looked up, saw the patch I'd installed still held, but with gaps around the edges.

We didn't have much time.

Odhran bowed his head to me before letting his gaze fall on Ameline. She didn't say anything to him, but he grimaced before taking his queen's hand.

"I had not thought to see you come to my border again," he said to the small girl body Ameline wore. "I believe I told you once if I found you here I would kill you."

Her smile was positively sweet. "And here we are," she said in her rich, deep voice, so creepy from the petite girl's mouth. "A pity you need me, isn't it?"

He met my eyes, shaking his head. "This is the only way?"

Sigh. I wished people would stop asking me that. Like I hadn't tried every other possible avenue first.

I almost missed the tension passing between the two sides of the Sidhe race, finally catching on when Charlotte chuffed at my side, head whipping back and forth. I turned from Odhran to see Aoilainn's people glaring with dark intent at the Unseelie people who glared right back.

"This is your doing." Leave it to Aoilainn to start pointing fingers. She did so, straight up at the gaping darkness on his side, the shining patch weakening by the second. "You have brought this on us."

"I have been fighting it since the moment it began," Odhran roared back, some of his vigor returning while Niamh snarled, her tall, slim body sheathed in black leather flashing with green fire. "It is you who refused to join forces with me, who refused to acknowledge we were losing our power to some outside source."

Aoilainn opened her mouth to argue. I very firmly closed it for her with a jab of magic.

"I don't care who kicked sand in whose face first," I said. "Or who bullied who six million years ago. Don't. Care." I poked my own finger at the swirling darkness, feeling the patch begin to give way, knowing we'd come just in time. "That? That matters."

"Why bother?" Ameline crossed her little arms over her chest and raised one eyebrow in artful disdain. "Perhaps we should let them be destroyed."

I almost agreed with her. Caught myself from doing just that.

"We need to act now." I gestured at the border, knowing as I think I'd known all along their own balance was out of kilter and made them vulnerable. "It's time that came down."

I watched the ruler's faces contort, centuries, millennia of disgust and opposition rising to spit out of them like venom. Even Odhran, who I knew understood just how close they were to destruction.

Only to feel the whole world shake beneath me as the patch above gave way with a vast, thundering boom.

Aoilainn instantly collapsed, sliding sideways from her horse as her Sidhe warriors fell to the ground. The pressure of the sudden exodus of magic drove the Unseelie to their knees, the king gasping as he reached out toward the border. Aoilainn's stubbornness shone in her face, even now.

"Mother," Shaylee spoke through my lips. "Live or die. Our race's fate is in your hands."

Aoilainn's will crumbled as she raised her hand and her power reached for the king.

And the border between the Seelie and Unseelie collapsed in a sigh of dying magic.

Our turn. I reached for Ameline's hand, felt her cold, firm child's fingers grip mine as our power, already bonded, surged between us at our touch.

Balance. Such a simple word to say. But finding it, grasping it, was a far more difficult matter. I was stronger than Ameline, that much was obvious. And she fought my strength even as the edge of the sky crumbled and the Sidhe realm began to fall into the gaping darkness. Back and forth Ameline and I fought while the world died.

Enough! I dropped my last defenses, pulled her to me. Felt her resistance fail and fall away. *There*, I sent to her, aiming us toward the gaping dark. *There is our enemy.*

Yes, she sent, coiling around me, feeding from my power as I fed from hers. *There.*

The core of the black called to me, pulled me forward, pulled us to it, swallowing us as we chased back through the shadowed sky to the source of destruction.

chapter thirty

I feared the black, remembering the devouring feeling of it the first time, when Demetrius led me to Wilhelm Castle. But this was different, whether because I was in control or due to Ameline's presence. I didn't suffer soul-eating terror from the crushing pull of the dark. This experience slid past smooth and quiet, like riding an underground river to our destination.

We emerged in a stone room, both of us stepping out together, hand in hand. Liander Belaisle hovered over a glass case, shimmering with the same iridescence as the magic Ameline and I wielded. He cried out as he saw us appear, real fear on his face, and rage.

A tall, stunning blonde stood next to him, her pale gray eyes flying wide as she pointed to us.

"No!"

But we were already acting, our power reaching for

the glass. A woman lay beneath it, prone and either dead or unconscious on a stone bed. I had no idea who she was or why the Sidhe magic was attracted to her, but she couldn't have it.

It didn't belong to her.

Calm settled over me, a detached sensation as all of my many parts formed one single soul. Power poured from me through the hand in mine and back again, the dark and light mingling in perfect harmony where we touched.

This must not be. The Dark spoke through Ameline.

Agreed. The Light sent, me and yet not me.

Together, power blazing, roaring through me like a freight train, Ameline and I raised our hands as one, gestured. The Light acted, making me feel like a patient passenger on this ride, though I was wide open and aware of everything happening to me, around me. The Dark formed a blade in the air, the Light crystalizing around it. Again we gestured while Belaisle's gaping black power rushed forward to consume us.

Our sword sliced through his magic, collapsed it into dust. Flashed in the candlelight of the stone room, whistling with the song of the maji veil as it rose and descended across the stream of green magic flowing forward to the glass case.

Cut off the suction of power gushing through the gap to the Sidhe realm.

The thunder clap in answer blew Belaisle back, tumbling him over and over until he crashed against the far wall and collapsed with a groan. The woman fell to her knees before being flung aside, landing next to him, his body cushioning her landing. Rage flared in her face as she struggled to rise.

"Damn you!" She crawled toward the woman under the shield. "If you've harmed Gaia—"

The Dark reached for the silent woman under glass, crushing power leveled to destroy her, but The Light stopped her.

Our work is done, It sent.

They feed her to support their efforts. The Dark's chilling gaze fell upon me, the ice blue eyes of Its host black and bottomless.

They fail. The Light felt along the edges of the case. *She will die and they will be left empty. But better to allow it to happen than to be the cause.*

The Dark paused. *You are certain?*

Flashes of images passed through my mind as the Light shared with the Dark. I caught brief glimpses of faces, Iepa and the tall blonde woman still panting on the floor, of Belaisle and a handsome young sorcerer, his power clear around him. Focused finally on a young woman, around my age who burned with amber fire.

The Dark sighed. *Agreed*, It sent.

I gasped out a breath as the Light retreated, feeling

Ameline's hand spasm in mine as the Dark left her. No time to hesitate, not when the bulk of Sidhe magic rose above us, hovering near the ceiling, writhing and spinning before slamming itself against the black hole it came through. A massive cascade of sparks flared, pattered to the floor as the Sidhe magic groaned its song in discordant despair.

We have to reverse the pull. I spun on the dark stain on the wall, the passage still open, though the pull had gone, no more magic entering. *Or all of this is for nothing.*

We have a chance to kill him. Ameline gestured at Belaisle.

No, the Light sent. *He is necessary. For now.*

No, the Dark agreed. *Not yet.*

Ameline's rebellion was clear on her face but I got the message. *I need you.*

She shook her head, but not in denial, dark regret on her face as we turned our backs on him and focused on the portal.

Simple really, this magic he'd created. Using the power of Sidhe souls he'd stolen, forming a wedge. The stolen spirits wailed their sadness at me, begged for release.

My sorcery devoured Belaisle's creation, drawing the black into me, shattering the edges of the opening. The wedge of souls collapsed, spinning into the center even as Ameline's power gobbled them up.

I didn't have time to share the horror I felt, to even

think about what she'd done. Not while Belaisle groaned behind me, muttered. The Light asked me to leave him alive, as much as I wanted to let Ameline kill him. And though I hoped listening was the right choice, I had to believe.

The Sidhe power cried out to me as I slashed open the veil between this plane and the realm. A clean, bright gash appeared, the shining light so different from the suctioning darkness. In one last clap of thunder rolling through me, rattling my teeth together, the power of the Sidhe flared and dove for home.

I spun to the touch of emptiness, felt it blocked even as Ameline lashed at Belaisle. He fell back again, eyes rolling into his head as he collapsed on the floor.

We were supposed to leave him alive. Why was I so worried? Wouldn't dead be better? A horrible chill raced up my back, fear like I'd never known. He was *necessary.*

I didn't kill him, Ameline sent. *But he'll find things have changed when he wakes.*

What the hell did that mean? No time to find out. As I opened my mouth to ask her out loud, chest tightening in anxiety, I felt myself being pulled into the tail of the stream of fleeing Sidhe magic. Reached out around Ameline's power toward the unconscious sorcerer only to feel my power slide over him, repelled by his magic.

His greatly reduced magic.

And then we were falling, back through the gap, the

Sidhe power gushing in a waterfall of green fire, plunging back toward the ground. We landed hard but intact, Ameline already pulling my attention upward, to the gap in the sky. The storm overhead rumbled, the clouds snapping in half, rain pouring down over us as I reached, Ameline reached. Together we plunged our creation magic into the torn lip of the Sidhe veil and repaired it.

I blinked into the suddenly blue sky, shaking water from my hair, storm gone, hole gone. Healed.

I spun to find Aoilainn watching me, as perfect and powerful as ever, Odhran and Niamh the same, their people restored. The realm repaired.

"I feared," Odhran said, coming to grip my shoulders in his hands, bending to kiss both of my cheeks. "But you did not fail us. Our thanks, Sydlynn Hayle."

Ameline scowled and looked away. I guess I understood her irritation at being left out of his gratitude, but she still hadn't thanked me for freeing her ass so I figured she could grovel a little before I felt bad for her about anything.

"What assurance do I have this won't happen again?" Just like Aoilainn to make this about her.

"You don't," I snapped. Blunt, yup yup. "But I can tell you this: if you work together from now on, the odds are much more in your favor."

Odhran grimaced, but nodded while Aoilainn gaped at me in horror.

"Surely you will now restore our border." She shook, braid vibrating over her shoulder, brushing the ground.

"Nope," I said, stepping away, feeling Charlotte come up beside me, the brush of her fur against my hand, Aoilainn's glamour firmly back in place. "You're just going to have to learn to get along."

Ameline was smiling again, clearly amused by the idea.

Like I gave a crap what she thought.

While Aoilainn spluttered and trembled, Odhran watching me with hooded eyes telling me he was now reconsidering his gratitude, I turned and marched off without another word. Charlotte kept pace, Ameline hurrying to catch up. I found myself smirking at her as she was forced to run a few steps, long hair bobbing behind her.

Yeah, she loved looking like a little kid. I could just tell.

I turned at the sound of my name, found Thalion striding forward to join us. The two Sidhe peoples milled around behind us, as though unsure about what to do next, though I was gratified to see Odhran and Aoilainn come together in the middle and touch hands.

Good enough. I'd saved them, but it was their responsibility to keep things in balance from now on.

Sheesh. I was going to come to hate that word.

"I will escort you," Thalion said. Paused. "If you wish."

Holy crap. Did we just save the entire of the Sidhe realm? A rush of giddy happiness flooded me, so much I smiled and hooked my arm through Thalion's, much to his shock.

"I wish," I said. "Thanks for the offer."

Ameline grumbled something under her breath and stomped faster, leaving us to follow her. I didn't even have to ask Charlotte to keep pace with the girl, though thanks to the connection we still shared, I could feel Ameline's frustration at being ignored. Treated like a kid.

A bubbling rage built inside her and I knew I'd have to watch her carefully.

"She is not to be trusted." Thalion's voice broke my concentration, but reinforced my worry.

"News flash," I said. Grinned at his eyebrow quirk. "Sorry. Yeah, I know that already." And yet, she'd done what needed doing. Proved she would stand against the Brotherhood. I briefly considered a visit to Belaisle, just Ameline and I, while the Gate loomed in the distance, rushing closer with every step.

That would be great, wouldn't it? Catch Belaisle in private and convince him to back off.

I'd even let Ameline be in charge of the convincing. Though the memory of his reduced magic stirred more anxiety. What had she done to him and where did his power go?

Hello, Syd. This wasn't rocket science. Ameline took

it. Going to have to talk to her about sharing.

"Keep us posted, would you?" I released Thalion's arm as Ameline paused in front of the gaping Gate. "Let me know if the Brotherhood decide to give it another try."

"I think we have less to worry about them," the prince said with a small smile, "and more concern my queen and the Unseelie king will come to blows."

Well, that was their business, now, wasn't it? First time I was happy to use Mom's company line.

"Sydlynn." Thalion squeezed my hand, his Sidhe power softer than I remembered. Come to think of it, he was, too. Not as coldly perfect as I remembered, more warm and open. "I have done things I'm ashamed of." He winced, still beautiful. "To Shaylee. And to you."

Um, wow. Empathy from a Sidhe? I loved the maji were wrong. Even the flawless Sidhe could grow hearts. I hugged him, let him feel Shaylee, our power wrapping around Thalion as he sighed in my ear.

"Friends," I said.

He smiled, a real smile, lighting his eyes as he kissed me gently on the cheek.

"My honor," he said.

I left him there, looking back over my shoulder at him as he continued to smile, one hand raised in farewell, remaining in that position until the Gate closed and he vanished from view.

CHAPTER THIRTY ONE

Liam's arms warmed me up as his earth magic grounded me. It was hard to enjoy with Ameline tied to me, but I did my best.

Now what? His mind caressed mine gently. *Are you taking her back?*

To prison. To the stronghold and her cell.

I wished.

I can't. I looked up into his eyes, welcomed the soft kiss he planted on my lips. *As much as I hate to admit it, we need her. And she has to be free to develop her power.*

"Happy to hear you've come to your senses." Ameline had to be eavesdropping. Gross. "That you finally admit we're on the same side."

"For now." I stepped away from Liam, felt his tension as he hovered over me, protective though he would never stand against her. "But what happens when the

Brotherhood is defeated?"

"I suppose we'll have to have that conversation when it happens." Ameline's chill smile turned my stomach.

Lovely.

"And Belaisle's magic?" My power prodded hers but she blocked me, at least as much as she could around the bond. "If we're going to have balance, you need to share."

"Actually," she said with her icy smile, "the magic I took from him, from his feeble followers, has brought us to equal."

She let me in then, allowed me to feel her sorcery, the blossom of her own.

Only took me a heartbeat to realize she was right. How much did that suck?

"You can leave her here." Liam's big hand settled on my shoulder. "I'm sure Galleytrot and I could find a cubbyhole to stash her in."

Appealing, her smushed into a stone closet. In the dark.

"She has to come with me." I stepped away from my Sidhe friend and squared off with Ameline. "At least for as long as she behaves herself."

Her smile didn't budge.

Without another option, knowing I was nuts and probably about to be murdered by my own family for even considering the possibility, I parted the veil, one hand holding Charlotte's, the other grasping a fist full of Ameline's Enforcer robe and took us home.

We appeared in the kitchen, again to my surprise, sliding right through the family wards. I'd never been able to do that before, usually forced to land on the edge of the park, near the back yard. I think our arrival was as shocking to the inhabitants of the kitchen as it was to me, because it took Gram and Sassafras a whole ten seconds before they started screaming at me.

Charlotte eased out from the line of fire as Shenka hugged herself, face twisting in a mix of fear and resolve. Only Trill seemed calm, sitting back in her chair, observing with a slight tilt to her head as Gram and my demon cat tore me a new one.

"What, by the blessed elements, were you thinking bringing her here?"

"Are you completely out of your mind or did you leave part of it behind when you ran off earlier?"

I let them rattle on, swear words popping out here and there as they yelled over each other to the point I couldn't make them out anymore. When Gram paused to take a breath, I cracked a whip of power in the air. They both fell silent, though from the shuffling fury of Gram's feet and the way Sassy's tail thrashed against the table I knew I had only seconds before they started up again.

"I know," I said, keeping my tone reasonable. "I do. But where else was I going to take her?"

Gram grumbled while Sassafras whined low in his throat.

"Pretty." Only then did I notice Demetrius, tucked into the corner, staring at Ameline through the crystal he held to his eye. He bent his head then, looking around it. "Not so pretty."

Would have been funny. Actually, really was. I snorted before I could stop myself, triggering a giggle fit from the little sorcerer. He pattered his feet on the floor, looking at Ameline through the crystal again.

Gram eased up then, thin arms crossed over her chest. Even Sassafras seemed to relent, though it took a while for his puffed up fur to fall back to normal.

"What a lovely welcome." Ameline's mouth twisted in a sneer. Before anyone could stop her, she stepped forward and took a seat. Mine. Did she know I usually sat there or was it just her innate gift of pissing me off? "I'm hungry." She snapped her fingers at Shenka. "Fix me something."

Oh no, she did *not*.

But I didn't get to react. Before I could say anything, shoot her down, Gram's hand snaked out and smacked Ameline on the back of the head so hard her chin hit her chest.

"Manners," Gram said, baring her teeth in a nasty smile.

Ameline snarled back before shrugging. "You'll pay

for that, you old bitch."

I jerked on the power connecting me to Ameline, so hard the chair she sat in slid back a few inches. "Enough," I said. "Or you're going back to prison after all."

All civil then? Grand.

Shenka did end up making Ameline a sandwich, but as the dark maji ate it I couldn't help but hope my second found a way to spit in it first. Childish? Yeah. Still.

No one treated Shenka that way. Or threatened my grandmother.

I told them about the Sidhe, apologizing to Gram about Varity. Felt a chill of worry no one had come to arrest me yet. But when I turned to Charlotte, she shrugged.

"I didn't hit her that hard," the weregirl said. Gram scowled at her before Charlotte winced. "At least, I didn't think so."

"You realize what this means." Sassafras hadn't touched his tuna. A testament to how upset he was. He never turned his nose up at tuna. "They'll be coming for you." He looked sideways at Ameline who continued to eat her lunch without a flicker of acknowledgment. "For both of you."

It wasn't like I didn't know there would be consequences to my actions. "I know," I said, sagging back into my seat. "We'll run before they come."

Just the thought made me cringe inside. Why had I

brought her here? I was putting the whole family at risk by sitting here, eating lunch like nothing happened.

Like I hadn't condemned myself to die.

Explaining about the maji took a little more time, though I carefully left out the part about Ameline's heritage. She turned to meet my eyes, face blank, but didn't question me when I kept that little secret.

I'd rather she didn't know. Not that Ameline cared even a scrap about Gram's feelings.

As you wish, she sent.

Why didn't I trust her to keep her mouth shut?

Demetrius finished his sandwich, mushing his crusts together into a solid chunk before stuffing it into his mouth. I remembered his mission and cringed at the thought of asking.

"Alison?" I leaned toward him, his blue eyes lifting from his milk glass to meet mine.

"Gone," he said. "Bu-bye."

Damn it. I'd have to deal with her eventually.

"She knows," he said. "About the gem."

What gem?

Oh hell.

I'd forgotten all about the jewel in my pocket. Had carried it with me through all of the mess I'd just survived. My fingers fished it out before I considered the company I was in. Ameline leaned forward, eyes intent on the black stone in my palm.

"Is that the taint?" So she knew about the vampires, too, did she? Seemed her maji guide was more forthcoming with information than mine.

Iepa would be hearing about that.

I pulled my hand back, out of her reach, closing my hand around the jewel. "I have to destroy it." She'd already managed to gain enough sorcery to equal me in the last little bit. No way was I handing her the means to match my vampire essence on a silver platter.

And yet, wasn't that the point?

Sigh.

Ameline's eyes narrowed. "You know you need to give it to me," she said. "My development will be that much closer to complete. And to confronting the Brotherhood with the pair of us as equals."

Yeah, like that was going to happen.

It's actually an excellent idea, my vampire sent. *Horrible to contemplate, but she's correct.*

"I'm happy to put off our final confrontation a little longer," I said, shoving the gem back in my pocket.

Ameline's lips bowed down into a pout, though her eyes flashed with anger.

"You're a fool," she said.

"Maybe," I said. "But I'd rather not give you access to unlimited vampire energy at the moment. Especially not the damaged kind."

"You can't let it fall into the Enforcer's hands, either."

Trill's dark eyes shone with worry. "It has to be destroyed, Syd."

Great. "We're going on the run," I said. "I'll handle it when I get a minute."

Speaking of which, I'd put off our departure long enough. Pushed the limits of what was reasonable into the ridiculous. They'd be coming for me, any second now.

Time to go.

The moment I stood, backed away from the table, cold air enveloped me. I cried out from the chill, my skin burning from the icy touch, just as someone giggled maniacally in my ear. I felt ghostly fingers in my pocket, grasped for her, too late.

Too late.

Alison flared to life next to me, the gem in her grip.

Grinned and vanished.

And I, without thinking, went after her.

Alone.

Chased her through the edge of the family territory, felt the startled touch of Enforcers before flashing into the veil again, lunging after Alison. Brushed over her echo as she plunged into the ground.

Into the cave where my elemental magic wouldn't work.

Furious, raging, I went after her.

My maji power dimmed, but stayed with me, as I dove beneath the earth and emerged in a burst of exploding fire, into the inner chamber. Alison crouched over a stone, the gem lying there, power hovering in her hands.

I reached for the gem, knowing there was nothing I could do, felt her undead energy reach it before mine, crack the seal, break it open.

Black mist poured up from the ground, groaning as it circled Alison before plunging into her ghostly form. I fought it, wrestled with all of my ability, but I was weakened by the loss of my elemental magic, the maji in me not yet fully formed, unable to push past the seals on the cavern.

Leaving the desperate, hungry magic to bond with the desperate, starving girl.

I knew it the moment she came to life again, felt her heart thud once in response, fall still. But just the sight of her, solid and real, hovering above the stone floor, her eyes blazing with white fire while the black pits devoured blue pounded a spike of fear inside me.

Not vampire, not human, not ghost. Something entirely different looked at me from behind Alison's face, laughed at me with Alison's voice.

"Perfect," she said, words echoing with power. "He was absolutely correct."

"Who?" I had to fight her, used my magic to seek a weak point only to have my vampire gasp and retreat at the touch of her.

So evil, she whispered. *Syd, we're in trouble.*

Alison laughed again, floating closer. The scent of decay she'd carried with her was gone, replaced by the haunting aroma of Alison's old favorite perfume and the faintest whiff of alcohol. Weird how the smells triggered a reaction in me. Loss and guilt and so much grief I choked.

"You know who," Alison said. Lunged for me only to fly back as my maji power repelled her. She snarled, looked down at her hands. "Whole again," she said. "Has its disadvantages."

Which meant she could be trapped, captured. But even as I lashed out with my power, I felt her slip through my hold, her shielding slithering, slick and oily, as she rose higher. I grasped for her over and over again, pulling, tearing at her, unable to keep a grip as she began to glow.

"Liander Belaisle sends his regards," Alison said before flashing over into a sunburst and vanishing.

I tucked my chin, covering my face with my hands to shield from the light, cursing as I reached for the veil to go after her.

Syd! Gram's mind latched onto mine, the barest touch of her making it through the blocking on the elements. *Syd!*

Gram? I tore at the veil, thoughts of Alison gone, desperation and absolute terror stopping my own heart. *GRAM!* I lunged for home.

Even as I felt my grandmother fall.

chapter thirty two

Panic tore a hole inside me, drove me to abandon Alison, abandon my own sense of safety, pushing me to run for the house.

To Gram.

Who I couldn't feel anymore.

It wasn't until I crossed through the family wards her power touched mine again. But dim, so dim, and failing by the moment. I couldn't think, breathe, speak as I rushed through the empty house to the back door.

Into carnage.

Charlotte lay sprawled on her face, half inside the house, cheek and bleeding nose pressed to the stone of the walk way. Shenka sagged on the grass nearby, passed out, skin so pale I thought she was gone.

Two black-robed Enforcers lay just past her, bodies smoking, the scent of burning flesh slapping me in the face.

But I didn't focus on them, not while my eyes flashed over their dead bodies.

To the limp old woman collapsed in the grass.

I ran to her, fell on my knees, pulled Gram's body into my lap, screamed a sob as I poured power into her. She was so far away, felt like Galleytrot did when Ameline took his power. Like Charlotte had when she almost died.

But this was Gram, powerful, unstoppable. Invincible like me.

She had to be.

Had to.

I felt her fighting to come back to me, latched onto her, pulled her up from the black threatening to smother her and steal her soul. Her chest rose in a gasp, eyelids fluttering, power returning slowly, oh so slowly, even the Sidhe soul inside her fought for life.

I gave her everything I had. Vampire, demon, Sidhe, witch. Used sorcery to drain the life force from the very ground beneath me, forced it into Gram. Ignored the feeling of the Wild Hunt stirring as I disturbed their rest.

Let them rise. If Gram died—

No.

Never.

"Syd!" I didn't move when I heard Trill call my name, felt her next to me as she fell beside me, reached for Gram. "Syd, what happened?"

"You were here!" I spun on the maji girl, fury and terror cutting giant gashes in my soul. "Why did you let this happen?"

Not her fault. So not. Mine. All mine. Trill's face crumbled as she stroked Gram's forehead.

"Ameline," she whispered.

Ameline.

She would die. And I would be happy to kill her.

Gram's pulse sped up, power gushing out of her like an open wound. I hunted for the gash, tried to seal it. Felt Ameline's power in the way.

Lashed at her, even as the pain of hurting her sliced more ribbons of agony.

I told her, Ameline sent, cold and detached, a clinical observer of my grandmother's weakness. She'd already taken one from me.

This one she could not have.

Light and Dark, balance or not, I drove my power into her, felt her collapse under the assault, writhe free like a snake with a snarl of rage.

Save her then, if you must. But I'll see you again, Sydlynn Hayle. When the time comes.

Bitch. I threw myself at her through our connection, felt her sever it.

No time to chase her. No time while Gram was dying in my arms.

The memory of holding Ahbi, of feeling her blood

on my hands, how her body went limp, the last breath of life escaping tore a giant sob from me.

Nononononono. NO.

I spun down into the darkness trying to take Gram away from me. Clawed my way to a stop, pulled myself out. And brought my grandmother with me.

I blinked away tears, panting for breath. Reached for the one person who could help me save Gram who still fluttered, weak and lost.

MOM!

She came to me, in a rush of power, flaring blue magic bursting overhead. Mom's magic met mine. Yes, she was here, we would save Gram now, go after Ameline together and everything would be fine—

The Council power grasped me and jerked me back from Gram, slamming me into the ground.

No, what was she doing? Incoherent screams escaped me as I fought with my body, unable to focus my power away from Gram as I tried to support her, felt Mom cut me off. Off. Over and over I tried to reach Gram, only to have the Council's full power pin me as Mom came to stand over me, fury vibrating from her.

I couldn't even bring myself to use my magic against her, still battering the edges of her wards around Gram. I had to save her.

Please, just let me save her.

"Sydlynn Hayle," Mom said in a voice shaking with

rage. "You are under arrest for freeing Ameline Benoit from prison."

What the hell was wrong with her? "Mom!" I barely pushed enough air out of my straining lungs to speak, gathered my mind to string words together. "Gram needs help. Please."

Varity appeared next to Gram, bent over her, face grim and tears on her cheeks. When she met my eyes, hers were full of hate.

"Where is Ameline?" Mom's sharp question distracted me.

"Help Gram!" I fought harder, feeling my maji power rise, the swelling of my sorcery begging to absorb the magic holding me down. But I didn't care about me, not now. Not while my grandmother lay limp and unresponsive, her power link to mine so weak I could barely feel her at all. "Mom, you can't let her go!"

The Council power wrenched me to my feet, two Enforcers securing me between them.

"Take her," Mom said, disgust and rage washing over me as she sliced open the veil.

No. Not this way. I had to save Gram—

Something dove past my shielding, already gaping wide thanks to my grief, and struck me so hard the world went black.

I spiraled into it, falling and sobbing, still screaming her name.

chapter thirty three

They gave me Ameline's cell. Of course they did. I sat, dressed in a white robe just like hers, bare footed on the cold stone floor. My magic was intact, at least. They'd done nothing to block it off. Which made me wonder about the wards in the stronghold and why they weren't worried I'd bolt.

Which I planned to do. Eventually.

This time was very different from the last. No nice suite of rooms, no playing at "asking me questions." No fooling around with the coven leader who broke so many laws they probably didn't even need to hold a trial to sentence me to burn.

I really had to give up the family magic. Just freaking do it already. Before they held my continuing leadership against the coven. But I promised Sassafras I wouldn't, that I'd wait and talk to him first. And since I had no communication with the outside world...

Yeah. Who was I kidding? My reluctance had nothing to do with Sass. I was afraid, plain and simple. Not just for me, but for Shenka. And for Gram.

Gram. I could still feel her, at least. So she was alive and well. Or, alive, anyway. The rest would have to wait. Her touch was the only thing keeping me from busting out of here. Until I knew if she was going to be okay, I couldn't let go of the family magic. Because her part would leave with mine and for all I knew the coven's power was the only thing keeping Gram alive.

Because the elements knew I didn't do much to protect her, did I? Guilt gnawed in my guts, ate away at my strength. I'd left her there, abandoned her, Shenka, Charlotte. All of them. Allowed Ameline to hurt my family.

Only to fail, to watch Alison take the vampire taint into herself and become something I couldn't understand.

I had no idea how Charlotte was, if she recovered. Why the Enforcers had been in my yard. Even if the power I pulled from the ground meant big trouble with the Wild Hunt. Nothing, nada, zippo information. I'd woken in Ameline's—my—cell dressed as I was and with the fragile connection to Gram the only thing I could cling to.

And what did I have to show for Gram's harm, for

Charlotte's, Shenka's. For the loss of the two Enforcers? Nothing. Worse than nothing.

Alison was real, full of the vampire taint and working for the Brotherhood.

I ground away at my own spirit, winding up the same guilt again and again, crushing myself with loathing and regret.

Where was Iepa in all this? She allowed it to happen as much as I did. Hate blossomed, peaked in my chest, burned me with its power. She abandoned me after telling me I needed Ameline. Forced my hand. And now that everything had taken a fast train to apocalypse, she was nowhere to be found.

Typical.

I gritted my teeth against the internal battering.

To hell with her. With the so-called prophecy, my destiny, all of it.

I was so done.

I thought the time alone in my cell would be quiet. For peaceful contemplation of my impending doom. Lots of emptiness I could use to beat myself further.

Not so much.

The cell door swung open shortly after I crossed my arms over my chest and told myself no matter what happened the world could fall apart and I wouldn't lift a finger to help from now on. I contemplated my escape and subsequent hiding out in a cave somewhere no one would find me when Pender entered, a troubled look on his face.

"Coven Leader," he said. Licked his lips. I noticed he kept his distance, not leaving the vicinity of the door. Was he afraid of me?

Good. He should be.

"I'm here to take your statement." A glowing line of writing appeared next to him, tracing out his words in blue flame.

I turned my face away, calling up my shielding, opening the dark flower of my sorcery, ready to fight him off if he tried to make me talk.

And ignored him.

The silence held for a long time, his power probing mine until he sighed. Left the room, closing the door behind him.

Didn't try very hard. Which made me wonder. But my deep-seated depression shoved curiosity away.

Who cared? He'd either be back with a pack of bullies to force the issue or not.

Shrug.

My vampire whispered to me I was acting quite childishly, but I smothered her. And my demon who snarled in answer. Shaylee when she tried to prod me to act. The family magic mourned with me, so I didn't have a fight there. And my sorcery? Well, it begged and pleaded to be let out, to sample the magic of the stronghold. Which told me in no uncertain terms if I tried to use power outside of my personal shields I'd probably set of a chain reaction the likes of which I'd better be prepared for.

Not yet.

My second visitor appeared only a few minutes later. Erica came to sit beside me while I fought the trembling taking me over at the sight of her sad face.

"Gram?" I clutched at Erica's hands, felt how hot hers were, looked down to see mine were white and shaking.

"I don't know," she said. "Syd, what happened?"

I shook my head. "I need to know if Gram's okay."

Erica sat back, sighed, rubbing her tired face with one hand, still holding onto me with the other. "Miriam won't tell me anything," she said. "I'm worried about her, Syd." She squeezed my fingers. "And you."

"I'm fine," I said. "Go take care of Gram."

Erica left, shoulders bowed while I raged inside.

Mom. Damn her. Had she left Gram to suffer?

I felt power appear in the room, lurched to my feet, turned to face Iepa with a snarl on my lips. Threw all of the venom and hate simmering inside directly at the maji who trembled as I spoke.

"Get out." I advanced on her, voice rising to a roar. "NOW!"

Iepa raised one hand to me. "I'm sorry this is

necessary—"

I called her a very bad word even as my maji power flared against her.

With guilt collapsing her features, Iepa tore open the veil and vanished through it.

Screw. Her.

I turned my back, felt the veil part again, spun to scream bloody murder at her if not commit it.

To have Meira stumble into me with a cry.

chapter thirty four

I held her against me a moment before pushing my sister out to arm's length. "What are you doing here?"

"Syd." Meira clutched at me, face younger only because of her obvious fear. "We have to get you out of here." She tugged on me, pulling me with her, toward the wavering slice in the veil still gaping behind her.

I slipped free, shaking my head. "I can't go," I said. "Not until I know if Gram is okay."

Meira's lips trembled. "Do you have any idea how much power it took to reach you? To cross?" She wrung her hands at me. "Grandmother is helping, but she won't be able to hold it forever. The power of the stronghold is fighting her. We have to go now."

"Meems." I hesitated. Maybe going with her was a good idea. We could sort out all the mess later, after I'd had time to think.

No. I couldn't abandon Gram. Even if that meant the Council managed to tie me to a stake and set me on fire.

"I have a plan," I said. Not much of one. But there was enough truth in what I said I was able to smile at my sister, to hug her again. To appreciate the love she poured over me. "I promise, I'll be fine."

Meira nodded against my shoulder before backing up. Wiping her nose on her sleeve, amber eyes welling with more tears.

"That's why you're my hero," she whispered before spinning and plunging into the veil just as it snapped shut behind her.

Hero? Me?

Wow, kid had some serious issues to work out if I was her role model.

I sat on the end of the narrow bed, feeling worse for having seen Meira, for some reason. Maybe because I really was alone in this, and knew it now. No rescue. Yes, I could run. Would when the time came. But I refused to take anyone else down with me.

Visitor number five shocked me so much when she stormed through the door I almost forgot to ask about Gram.

"Mom." I gasped out her name, stumbled to my feet as my mother slammed the door behind her and turned to glare at me.

"You will give a statement," she snarled, power

crawling around her like a living thing. "You will confess to freeing Ameline Benoit." Her fingers crept to her neck, clutched at it. "You will be punished for your crimes." Her hand scrabbled as though searching for something even as she choked on her words.

No necklace. She'd lost her pentagram long ago, back when she'd first become Council Leader. And though Meira and I had a new one made for her, infused it with our magic, she'd never worn it. At least to my knowledge.

And this wasn't the first time I'd seen her claw at her neck like that. I let my power out, touched Mom with it, felt the emptiness before the Council power crashed against me.

"You dare, criminal?" Spittle flew from Mom's lips as she stormed to face me, both hands on her throat now. "You will burn on a pyre and your bones will be crushed to dust!"

Holy. Freaking. Crap. Council magic or not, this was not my mother.

Was. Not.

My eyes fell to her hands, so desperate around her neck. "Mom," I said, stomach lurching as I made a connection in my head. "Where is the necklace I gave you?"

Mom's eyes bulged, her breath coming in short gasps. "You will confess," she said. Barked out.

I was an idiot. A total, complete idiot. Blamed the

influence of the Council power for Mom's shift. I'd wondered once if a darker power was to blame, but when I'd felt the pressure she was under, the push of the Council magic, I'd allowed myself to believe that was the reason she'd become someone I didn't know anymore.

But the emptiness I felt around her, every time I touched her, just before her magic rejected me. That wasn't witch magic.

How had I missed it?

Mom spun away from me, body convulsing as she bent over, gasping for air even as she repeated, "you will," like some kind of mantra.

My heart breaking, I raised my hands to my own neck and slid free the pentagram necklace she'd given me. They'd left it with me, for whatever reason. And I was grateful. Because her power sat embedded in it, and a spell of protection, one she'd tried for years to make me wear. Something I'd only done recently.

The same as hers, made by *her* mother.

As Mom straightened, her back still to me, I stepped into her space. She spun, eyes bloodshot and face crimson from an internal battle I could only begin to imagine. Before she could stop me, I lifted the necklace over her head, sliver sliding through my fingers as I whispered power into the metal and dropped the pentagram pendant around her neck.

chapter thirty five

I'm not sure what I expected to happen. Nothing, maybe. But certainly not the pulse of power that rippled out from Mom in a sonic blast, rocking through me as I held onto her for balance and she to me.

Her transformation happened almost instantaneously, though I had time to watch her shift in the heartbeats between. How her skin faded to a more normal hue, deep wrinkles plumping and vanishing as her youthful appearance returned. The way the silver traces in her hair flashed before darkening back to black. But it was her eyes, the deep blue of them, once tormented and full of rage that changed the most.

Mom's hands squeezed my shoulders as the last of the power wave left her, those beautiful eyes welling with tears. One hand lifted to her throat, to the pentagram necklace, before touching my cheek so gently I barely felt the pressure of her skin.

"Syd?"

I sobbed once, flooded with relief, almost knocking me over as I reached for her, pulling her against me. My mom. My mom was back and that was all that mattered.

She wept with me as we clung to each other like little girls who'd seen the Boogeyman, the scent of her lilac perfume once almost rancid now pure and clean again. Filling me with a sense of absolute peace and so much joy I wanted to jump up and down and clap my hands.

And hug her forever.

Mom finally released me, face now as flawless as I remembered, so young again I almost did a double take, wondering if I'd somehow found a mirror, we looked so much alike. I kissed her cheek, laughing as I cried, unable to speak just yet, but knowing from the touch of her power she was clean and whole and herself again.

She led me to the bed, sat next to me, hands shaking so much I clutched them between mine to steady us both.

"Syd," Mom whispered. "Oh, Syd." She touched the necklace again, fingers gripping it so tightly they turned white. "What have I done?"

"Nothing," I said, a little surprised by the snarl in my tone. "Not you, Mom."

She shook her head, brows coming together, eyes haunted as she drew a panicked breath. "I fought so hard." Mom gasped for air, chest hitching. "Syd, I fought and I fought, but I couldn't break free. I knew what was happening, but there was nothing..." she choked off, hugged me again. "I almost destroyed us all."

"Not you," I repeated. "The Brotherhood."

She sat back, hand finally dropping the pentagram to her chest where it glowed softly with blue power. Her power. And mine as a shimmer of iridescence raced over it. "How did you know?"

"Sorcerers use the inherent magic in objects to gain power." I'd done so myself just recently. To save Gram. "They must have stolen your pentagram. Remember Margaret's ring?" The leader of the European Council admitted the Brotherhood tainted her through the ring she'd worn. "Mom, I should have known, but the Council power wouldn't let me look closely." It hovered inside her now, calm and relaxed, a tame lion ready to pounce. "They must have used your pentagram to control you and, through you, the Council's magic."

Mom shuddered before rising to pace. "I've failed," she said.

I couldn't have her crumble on me now. "Mom." She turned to face me. So beautiful I smiled, beamed. I had my mom back, damn it. How awesome was that? "Listen to me. The Brotherhood is insidious." Had proved it so many times I could hardly count. "The most important thing is you're free. And so is the Council power."

It made so much sense to me now, Mom's mood

swings, the way she seemed to struggle against her own will. Not the Council magic, but the Brotherhood's manipulation.

"They will know by now you're free," I said. "We have to put up safeguards to make sure you stay that way."

Mom sat with me again, hands holding mine, face composed, though a deep hurt still shone in her eyes. "The Council," she said. "They will all need to be tested." Her innate sense of responsibility kicked in, visible in the set of her shoulders, the determination on her face. "And dealt with if they are also under control." She shook her head, dark hair swinging. "How could I have let this happen?"

Wow, that sounded familiar.

"They tried to break you by inches," I said. Knew it was true. Recalled Mom's slow deterioration up to this point. "You wouldn't have felt it at first, since their power is empty to you. Bits and pieces, influencing you on choices you normally wouldn't have made." Now I knew it, I could feel it, see it in everything she did, right from my first day at Harvard. "I'm as much to blame as you are. More. I have sorcery. I should have recognized their influence for what it is and acted a long time ago. But I thought it was the Council power controlling you and knew you'd never give it up."

Mom nodded, lips thinned in anxiety. "You're right," she said. "Syd, I was so close to breaking."

250

I squeezed her hands. "But you didn't." I laughed again. "I bet they didn't factor in just how freaking strong you are, Mom." Her blue eyes glistened with more tears, but she listened. "I'd love to know how many sorcerers *you* broke before they managed to make you do anything."

Her mouth turned up into a little smile. "I hope it hurt," she said.

That was my mom, all right.

Mom's little moment of vengeance died when she gasped and paled. "We have to get you out of here."

Oh, now she remembered I was in prison.

"I don't know how." She might as well have the truth. "Mom—"

She shushed me immediately. "I'm here to take your statement," she said. "Since you are unwilling to give it, I have no choice but to leave."

Rules. Laws. Okay then.

"Mom," I said, feeling my own desperation rise, though not for me. "Gram?"

She hesitated. But when she answered, it wasn't with bad news, just uncertain.

"I don't know," she said, grief coming back. "I think I sent the Kennecott twins to her." I liked them both, trusted them, knew Lula and Phon would take as good of care with Gram as they had with Liam when Ameline stole his Sidhe soul. Mom swept to her feet, pulling me up with her. "I'm going to go home and check on her now." She hesitated before hugging me again. But this time without fear, no longer shaking. When she leaned back and met my eyes, a powerful Council Leader looked back.

"We'll find a way to free you," she said, "if it's my last act as leader of the High Council."

She reached around her neck for the chain to my necklace, but I shook my head with a grin.

"I'm good," I said. "You need it more than I do."

Mom kissed my cheek gently before embracing me with her magic as she strode out the door, calling for Pender.

chapter thirty six

Maybe I shouldn't have been so optimistic, but knowing Mom was going to be okay, that she was finally herself, went a long way to making me feel better.

While I still didn't believe she would be able to save me from being condemned to death, at least she was whole and could help Gram. And Shenka when the time came I had to release the family magic.

I kicked myself for not filling Mom in on everything that happened, but since she seemed to think I had to stay quiet in order for her to do what was necessary, spilling the beans would have to wait. I could only hope Demetrius would think to warn Sunny about Alison. If his brain was even firing on partial neurons at the moment.

I paced, struggling with the knowledge it was likely Margaret Applegate never really left the control of the

Brotherhood. I certainly wouldn't put it past them to try to snare her again and piled on another coating of guilt I hadn't checked in.

You do realize most of what you're beating yourself up about really isn't your responsibility? My vampire's gentle hug went a long way to helping me shed the pressure of regret.

You warned them, my demon snarled. *They did nothing while we put our lives on the line for them. And that makes you guilty?* Her internal snort was accompanied by a blast of demon fire warming my insides.

It is their failing, Shaylee sent. *We have saved them so many times, perhaps they need to fall in order to understand just what it is they face.*

Hopefully the Sidhe had the message now. But I wasn't holding my breath. *It's always easier to blame the messenger*, I sent, glum.

Indeed, my vampire sent. *And for the messenger to do the same.*

Got it. Shake it off, Hayle.

I went to the tall, narrow window and stared out into the barren landscape, the dark gray sky matching my mood no matter how much I tried to convince myself I'd done the right thing. Of course I had. But the inevitable consequences almost did me in.

What would I do without my family? I'd fought being part of the coven most of my life. But now? Now I cherished them, each of them. Even more, I cherished my connection to the family magic, full of centuries of history and the power of dozens of witch leaders, even those before my line took over. What would my ancestors have done? If this were Thaddea Hayle, our first family leader, or her daughter, Auburdeen who Sassafras spoke so highly of?

I wished I knew.

It didn't help I stared out into the very place the battle between magicks was destined to take place. The last stand of witches, demons, Sidhe and vampires against the sorcerers.

It doesn't have to be this way. Iepa's mental touch was gentle, kind and hesitant, as though she expected me to give her the boot again. I almost did.

Almost.

Explain. Abrupt and rude? Hell yeah. She had a long way to go to earn my respect back.

When the time comes, she sent. *If you are willing, this can be decided another way. Among the four.*

News to me. *Then why all the doom and gloom battle for the fate of everything crap you've been drilling into me for so long?* Temper, temper. Screw that.

She was silent so long I thought she'd left and jumped a little when she did speak. *Our side has rules,* she sent. *The other doesn't follow them.*

Typical. *So break them,* I sent. Blunt was my only option at this point.

Again silence. A sigh. *Be well*, she sent and left me.

As frustrated as ever.

At least now we know more than we did before. My vampire was nothing if not practical.

My demon, on the other hand, snarled her irritation while Shaylee pouted.

I was with them, frankly.

Maybe we should just run. I slid my arms around myself, the soft fabric of my robe so thin I felt a chill despite the steady temperature of the room. More from the thought of acting than any shift in the weather.

Perhaps, my vampire sent. *Though it would be easier to do so once we are out of this plane.*

Not so sure, I sent. *We've been riding the veil through some powerful magicks lately.*

You don't have your crystal. My demon's grumbling flared with anger. *The Enforcers seized it, remember?*

True.

Patience, my vampire sent. *Your mother is whole again and has a great deal of power at her disposal. And we all know we will never allow them to kill us. The moment of choice will come. But it is not this moment.*

Was it wrong I was happy for the out?

I turned and crossed to the small desk, sitting on the low bench, fingers tapping on the wooden surface. The moment I touched it, I felt a breath of power. Not enough to stir the protections in the stronghold, clearly, but enough it woke my curiosity.

Carefully shielding my power, I let it slide out over the surface until it connected with a thin wisp of magic left behind.

Maji magic.

How ironic, Ameline's voice spoke in my head. *We've traded places. Because you failed to understand they will never let you do what you must. When you've had enough, break the chains holding you to their pathetic laws and come to me. To destiny.*

By the time her voice faded, my hands were clenched into fists so tight I was sure I'd find blood on my palms when I finally let them relax. Nope, just eight neat half circles of brilliant red fading fast as my maji heritage healed me before my eyes.

She knew. Expected me to get caught. Left me a message to taunt me.

Oh, I'd be coming to find her all right.

But she'd better look the hell *out*.

chapter thirty seven

Just as I was about to freak out from the solitude and my own spiraling thoughts, the seal around my door sighed and it opened. I braced myself, not sure who or what to expect. And winced at the sight of Varity Rhodes. She stared at me with a blank expression, draped in her heavy Enforcer robe, jaw tight, but eyes hooded and revealing nothing.

I felt terrible for what I'd been forced to do to her, thought of Charlotte and wondered if my poor bodywere was catatonic yet.

Before I could offer the apology I owed her, Varity spoke.

"Was it you who came to me?" Her voice seemed to echo in the stillness between us and I felt the brush of Enforcer power running beneath her words. "Was it you who asked me to bring you here?"

Um, weird question. I opened my mouth to confess.

Felt a jab from a place I wasn't expecting.

Lie, Quaid sent. *Lie your face off. Just do it.*

Huh? Okay, confused.

Tell her you have no idea what she's talking about. Quaid's deep voice was edged with desperation. *Don't argue with me.*

My temper flared. Bossy pants.

Syd, he snarled. *Don't be an idiot.*

Fine. But he'd pay for it later.

While I was getting much better at lying when it meant saving the world, lying to cover my own ass still gave me problems. I shrugged and went for nonchalant while my vampire sighed her disgust and took over.

"I don't know why I'm here," my vampire said, keeping my face straight. While I cringed inside for the untruth. Jeeze, even to save my life I was a goody two shoes. Sad, really. My vampire hissed at me before going on. "And I have no idea what you're talking about."

Varity relaxed suddenly, her power retreating, the empty look on her face easing. She didn't exactly smile, but the cold contempt was gone and I took that as a win.

She left without a word, the wards resealing as she left.

Weird. But there had to be something behind it, didn't there? Though it was pretty obvious it had been me who approached her.

What was Mom up to?

And why did she recruit Quaid to help knowing it would get him in trouble?

The last thing I wanted was to put anyone else at risk. But I guessed the people I loved had other ideas and since I was locked up in here with no way to give them a hard time over it, I just had to yell at them for being stupid once I broke out.

No way this little plan would work. No way.

Syd. Quaid's voice reached me again, distant, faint. I tapped into our connection despite knowing it might trigger the protections surrounding the stronghold. But his power must have been enough to keep it quiet, because after a brief rumbling stir of the magic wards around my cell, everything went silent again.

Okay, so fill me in, please. I wished he was here. That I could hug him and kiss him. Taste his power, feel his body against mine. But the thin thread between us would have to do.

I don't know what you did to Miriam, he sent, excitement and tension coloring his mental voice, *but she's not the woman who went into your cell.*

He could say that again. *What is she doing?*

She has a plan, he sent. Paused. *So did I, but she wouldn't let me break you out after you turned Meira away.*

That was you. Of course it was. *You showed Meems how to find this plane.* Love surged, warmed me up, made tears prickle my eyes, throat tight and hot. *You idiot.*

He laughed in my head and my memory showed me his dark chocolate eyes, the flash of his white smile. *Someone had to do something.*

I have a plan of my own, I sent. *And I can break myself out, thanks. Without putting your head on the block with mine.*

Doesn't matter, Quaid sent. The intensity of the connection increased, his magic winding around me, pulling me close. *I can't let anything happen to you.*

He loved me, I knew it. Could feel it, embraced it as much as I sent my own love to him. And yet here we were, unable to be together. Would never be.

What the hell was wrong with us?

Just be careful, he sent, voice fading. *Syd, they're coming. You'll have to—*

His connection severed, though I could still feel him. But our little discussion was over.

Which left me wondering: I'd have to what?

When the door unsealed and Pender entered, followed by Santos Councilor Huan Wong, Rhodes Councilor Willa Rhodes and Hensley Councilor Lauren Noble, I understood his warning.

They'd come to ask me questions. And I had to lie again. Convince them of this new truth, that it wasn't me who'd corralled Varity into leading me to Ameline.

Yeah, hello crash and burn of epic proportions.

Don't be so cynical, my vampire sent, shoving me aside

just as my demon shouldered past me, Shaylee shunting me behind her until the three of their spirits stood in front of mine, their egos sharing my body.

Freaky. But not like I hadn't given up control before. I waited, the family magic winding around me like an eager cat, as Pender bowed to me and repeated Varity's question.

"Coven Leader," he said. "Did you manipulate one of our Enforcers to bring you here with the intent to free Ameline Benoit?"

The pressure of magic surrounded me, Council power seeping through my shields. On purpose, as my alter egos let them in. Showed them what they wanted the witches to see. Me, innocent.

"I did not, under any circumstances, coerce Enforcer Rhodes." That much was absolutely true. She brought me here of her own free will. Still, if I could help Varity, throwing around the coercion thing, maybe they would think by suggestion she'd acted out of magical influence. Since she was still walking around, had come to see me earlier, I could only imagine she was in the clear. Wouldn't hurt, though.

They waited while my vampire went on.

"Nor did I enter this place at any time prior to my arrest." Blatant lie number one. We'd been here twice already. "In fact, I have absolutely no idea why I'm being held and refuse to give a statement until I'm told what is going on." Blatant lies number two and three flowed from my lips so easily I cringed. They had to feel it. Had to know I was full of crap.

Hush, my vampire sent as my demon took over.

"Considering how horribly I've been treated in the past," she said with my mouth, "I am appalled such accusations led to my arrest without a single word of my crimes being declared to me."

Pender's head bobbed, cheeks dark red even as the Council members flushed.

"It was our understanding you freed Ameline Benoit from this very cell." Huan's round face tightened. "You deny this?"

"Absolutely and without question." That was Shaylee. And I realized then why they took turns. So the witches could feel all of my magicks. As proof I told the truth. Which meant I'd have to step up at some point.

Yikes.

"I would like to know," Shaylee said, "why I was not informed the witch who threatened my family's wellbeing was allowed to escape."

"Because we believed you freed her." Huan stumbled over the accusation, losing steam. But she quickly recovered, nostrils flaring as she set her jaw. "You're not working with Ameline to undermine witch power?"

That one I could answer 100% with honesty and did so.

"Never," I snapped. Yes, I was working with her, under duress. But the caveat? To undermine witches? They had no clue.

None.

They asked a few more questions, more of the same, twisting the words around until I finally turned my back on them.

"I'm done talking," I said. "You have your answers. Either accuse me of a crime I didn't commit or let me go."

They left without another word, though I felt Pender linger. But by the time I turned around, he was gone.

Not that his absence lasted long. I had just enough time to fret myself into chewing my nails to the quick before the door unsealed and Pender returned.

Smiling. Cell exit opened wide.

"Coven Leader," he said. "You're free to go."

Holy. It worked?

"With one request," he said. "The Council would speak with you."

Oh, I had some words for them. So that suited me just fine.

I wished I had time to change, or that Pender offered, instead of being swept from the cell and around the corner to a large doorway still in my flimsy robe. This had to be the main entry, no endless stairs for me this time. And waiting by the door, his hands clasped inside his black robe, stood Quaid.

"Enforcer Trainee Tinder has requested to escort you." Pender stepped aside. "Be well, Coven Leader."

I could have been rude. But Pender was only doing his job, following the orders of the Council. Still, I couldn't bring myself to smile or anything. I nodded to him with all the confidence I could muster, before the door swished open to reveal an elevator. A little shocking to find one in what amounted to a medieval fort, but I didn't question it.

Quaid entered beside me, the doors sliding shut behind us. As the small stone room descended, magic propelling us down and then sideways, he held still, silent. I almost reached for his power, but let him be, still amazed I'd somehow managed to get away with the one real crime I'd committed.

The doors slid open, a short hall with a large mirror on the other end waiting for us. I approached it, realized how pale I looked, how thin the fabric of my robe really was, saw my hip bones poking out, collarbone stark against my slight tan. I'd lost weight, gained a little height. Looked so much like Mom I smiled.

I could live with that. But somewhere along the line, I grew up.

Freaky.

I turned to Quaid just as he stepped into me, arms engulfing me, pulling me to his chest. I breathed in his scent, embraced the pulse of his power, the heat of the passion he held in his heart for me.

For me.

His mouth burned my lips, edges rough with beard scruff, hands buried in my hair as he almost lifted me bodily into him. I pushed closer, hands inside his robe, under his t-shirt, sliding over his hot skin. My fingers traced his ribs as I lost myself in his breath, his heartbeat, the taste of his tongue. He flinched as my hands brushed the waistband of his jeans, sliding under the lip of fabric to stroke the soft skin of his lower abdomen.

"Syd." He groaned my name into my mouth before crushing me against his chest. My lips locked on his throat, teeth nipping down to the base of his throat.

"Quaid."

Sigh.

Quaid.

We both stepped apart at the same moment. His dark eyes looked black, pupils dilated, breath coming in short pants, hands clenching and unclenching at his sides.

I felt thoroughly mussed and absolutely in need of him, but I smiled instead of trying to finish what we'd started. "Thank you," I whispered.

"I love you," he said. Spun and left me there.

I didn't blame him for walking away. We had no future, together at least. But for as long as possible, I would steal these moments with him and cherish them forever.

The mirror beckoned, wavering as I approached. I touched the cold glass, watched as it rippled like the surface of a pond disturbed by my touch. A permanent portal, had to be. Drawing a breath, I closed my eyes and stepped through—

—breathed air so heavy it choked me—

—stepped out into light. Opened my eyes. To my surprise, I stood in the middle of the Council chamber and, as I turned, I spotted Pender behind me. How he'd beaten Quaid and I to the mirror, I had no idea. But his hand slid a shard of glass into his robes just as I turned to look and I understood.

He carried the way to the stronghold with him. How many such portable portals existed?

And did I need to worry one might fall into the wrong hands?

Concerns for later. I spun back as Mom began to speak.

"Your High Council would like to offer up our most sincere apologies, Coven Leader." It was just so good to see her again, as her. Surreal, considering what she'd come through. I caught myself on the edge of a grin and pushed it down. "You were wrongfully accused of a heinous crime." She gestured and Varity came forward. "When Enforcer Rhodes told us you freed Ameline Benoit, we believed her."

"I believed as well," Varity said. "Please, forgive me for falling for such an evil deception."

Okay, something happened to make them wonder if it was me or not. But what?

"New evidence arose just recently," Mom said. "Proving you had nothing to do with Ameline's escape."

Which was?

Pender stepped forward this time, setting a small coin on the floor in front of me. I recognized the feeling of maji power as the coin began to glow and Ameline's image appeared.

"Fools," her magical hologram said, same icy stare, same arrogance coming through loud and clear. "Did you really think you could hold me? I am maji." Her glossy black hair tossed as she shook her head. "And while, if things were different, I would gladly allow Sydlynn Hayle to burn, she is necessary." Ameline's blue eyes blazed in the recording. "I hate to admit her power, but she has saved you countless times from destruction. And her reward? You treat her like a criminal." She laughed, cold and calculated to raise the most anger. I know it worked on me despite the message. "I'm shocked at your idiocy. How you would ever believe she would help me after our history is remarkable." I watched the faces of the Council, met Mom's eyes as Ameline's image wavered. "Hear me, you worthless witches. You will fall, and I will rejoice in your end. But if this plane, if all planes, are to survive, it's time to come together." She seemed to look right into my eyes. "I'll see you soon," she said.

And vanished.

As Pender bent to retrieve the coin, it flared once more before bursting into a puff of black smoke. I waved my hand under my nose at the stench even as my heart clenched in rage.

She saved my life. Again. Ameline thought I owed her, told me when she'd triggered my demon to rescue me from being drained by the vampires. And her little show gave me every indication she still thought so. Wanted to rub my nose in the fact I needed her.

I'd find her. And we'd see who needed who in the end.

chapter thirty eight

I thought that was it. Free to go, out of there. But Mom wasn't done.

Not by a long shot.

"Coven Leader Hayle," she said, voice ringing with authority. "With the recent attack on the Dumont coven and the escape of Ameline, we now clearly see the threat you've so patiently tried to warn us about." Snort. Good one, Mom. Because I was the queen of patience. "Your growing power and approaching status as maji gave us pause." Freaked them the hell out. She was good at this diplomatic speak. "But without your assistance, our covens would be under the control of sorcerers whose only interest is domination of all magicks."

Shocker. No one argued, turned red in the face. Nada.

Maybe I was wrong about the others being under the influence.

"Because of your special status," Mom said, "we, the North American High Council, grant you full immunity and impunity to act on any threat you see arise without compunction."

Did she just hand me the keys to the Universe?

"Terrible days lie behind us," Mom said. "And even worse lie ahead. Without you, we would fail and we know it." She sighed, sat back. "And that failing is mine."

Oh, crap. Don't tell me she was going to go all martyr on me all of a sudden?

Erica stared at Mom. "What are you saying?"

"For the last two years," Mom said in a low, level voice, "I have been under the control of the Brotherhood."

Silence. No outrage, no screaming. A little squirming.

They knew.

Because they were, too. I extended my energy, knowing now I had absolute freedom to do so and felt each and every one of them. Touched on the threads of emptiness leading away from them, some deeper and more seated than others, but none as controlled as Mom.

"Thanks to my lack of diligence," Mom said, "this Council has been manipulated by the very evil I sought to protect us from. And, because of that, I resign my position as leader of this Council."

Mom rose, gathering her magic, ready to force the Council power from her.

Like that was going to happen.

I slid a shield around her, maji magic sealing her tightly. She stared at me, frowning, but more from sadness than anger.

"In finding your freedom," I said, voice throbbing with emotion I couldn't contain, "you've become the very person we need the most." She trembled in my grip, eyes bright. "Now sit your ass down and listen."

She did. Amazing.

"Each of you has lost a personal item." There was no question now. The Council members exchanged curious looks. "Items embedded with your old family magic."

That got their attention. Erica reached for her wrist. Mom gave her a bracelet years ago. Missing. Huan Wong touched her earlobes, empty of adornment. The other Council members shifted uncomfortably, nodding agreement.

"The Brotherhood's power lies in manipulation and stealth." I didn't mean to pace, but it was hard to hold still with my mind whirling. "They use items embedded with family power to get to us." It was a theory, yes, but I think I'd proven it correct with Mom and thinking back to Margaret Applegate's ring, I knew I was right. "As important as those losses were, why were you unable to find them with magic? Magic you'd carried most of your lives?" None of them spoke, all pale, all quiet, eyes locked on me. Huan twitched, the emptiness around her tightening. Which meant we were being observed, didn't it?

Time to put an end to that.

I welcomed my dark blossom to open, felt the blackness gaping beneath me, allowed it to reach for the threads of sorcery tying the witches to their lost belongings. Traced the path back in a rush of darkness to the source. Not physically this time, there was no need for so small a job. But I felt him, Belaisle, the anchor. Felt his rage, heard his shriek of fury as I calmly severed his connections, sending each of them back with a crack, like a slap to his face.

The tokens I gathered in my power and destroyed. They were too tainted to return to their owners. I felt the remains of their magic trace back to their covens before retracting my awareness to the Council chamber again.

Each of the Council members looked shocked. As though I'd punched them in the gut. Erica sobbed once before covering her mouth with her hands. Huan spun in her seat and threw up rather noisily on the floor while Willa swooned and had to be supported by Lauren.

"You were all compromised," I said, but not to accuse them. Not in the least. This was my fault as much as anyone's. "But now that you are clean, you will stay that way." My maji power swelled, the sorcery inside me forming a slick skin around them, sealing them from outside magic. Even Mom who shuddered, but nodded.

"You can't step down now. Because we have no idea who else is under their influence."

Mom sighed deeply as the rest of the Council murmured their agreement.

"We've been presented an opportunity to act," Mom said. "To cleanse our covens of the influence of the Brotherhood once and for all." She clenched her hands before her. "And, when we're done, take this battle to them."

Mess #1 handled. About a gazillion to go.

chapter thirty nine

They wanted to talk, but I was done. I left them to hash out their own guilt and frustration while I finally let myself think of home.

And Gram.

Mom descended to my side, took my hand as I sliced open the veil and headed for Wilding Springs. Pressed my crystal into my palm as she did, returning it to me. The tiny soul inside rejoiced at our reunion, but I couldn't muster enthusiasm. Not when I didn't know what waited for me on the other end of the trip.

The kitchen felt surreal, like somewhere I remembered from a long time ago, but hadn't thought of in ages. Shenka dropped the carton of milk she held, the refrigerator door gaping open as she cried out and rushed to me, hugging me tight while a white pool of liquid spread beneath us.

"Syd," she whispered. "We were so worried."

I hugged her back, felt the touch of Mom's magic as she cleaned up the mess, looked up to see her put the milk back in the fridge. Shivered. She was herself, the woman I remembered when I was little. Young and fresh and so alive I could barely stand it. Seeing her like that, in our kitchen, made me feel sixteen again.

But I wasn't. And the world had changed so much since then.

I followed Shenka through the house, Mom behind me, holding my hand, to Gram's bedroom door. Two young witches were just emerging, whispering to themselves, but when Lula and Phon spotted me, they smiled.

And their smiles broke the dam I'd been holding my tears behind.

Lula hugged me kindly, Phon gently rubbing my back as I choked and tried to keep from collapsing into a puddle of soggy patheticness.

"She's resting," Lula said, hazel eyes kind, splash of freckles across her nose making her look younger than she was. "But I know she'll love to see you."

I wanted to ask a million questions, but they could wait. Gram was more important now.

The door creaked a little as I pushed against it, scrubbing the tears from my cheeks with the shoulder of my thin robe. Someone had pulled the curtains, casting the room in shadow and it took me a minute to adjust. A thin, frail shape lay under the sheets of my grandmother's bed, wispy white hair laid out on her pillow, tiny chest rising and falling in slow measure. Amber eyes shone as Sassafras lifted his head and looked up, his ears perked so far forward his whiskers quivered.

I hurried to the bed, trying to be quiet, feeling more sobs rising in my chest and fighting to keep them back so I wouldn't disturb Gram. She looked so different. Where Mom regained her youthfulness, her vigor, Gram looked like a shell of herself. Even when she'd been lost in madness, there was a robust feeling to my grandmother, like some giant lived in her wrinkled skin, just waiting to burst out.

Not now. Even her breath came in weak puffs through dry lips, her power lulled and transparent, as thin as her pale, pale skin.

I sank to the chair beside her bed, thinking of all the times I'd had to appease her with chocolate and tequila to keep her from blowing up the neighbors. How she'd always begged me to give back what I had of hers. Then, her happy cackle, the way her fuzzy socks carried her silently through her life. Stealth Gram with her pointy nails seeking out a rib, faded blue eyes sparkling in mirth, the crackle of her power, always there, always with me.

Soul sister.

Sassafras lay curled on her pillow, his cheek pressed to hers as he purred softly. I stroked his fur, kissed his paws, tears dripping onto his silver coat. I just couldn't hold them back anymore.

"I'm fine, girl." Her voice startled a meep out of me. "And so are you, it seems." Gram's eyes opened, fixed on me. A spark of hope rose in my chest as her power linked with mine. Until I felt her, how weak she was beneath the last of the family magic holding her to me.

My fault.

All my fault.

The family power coiled inside her, the remains of our shared magic humming softly, though it felt as diminished as she did. Her Sidhe soul sighed as Shaylee embraced her, replenished her. At least the gaping wound sealed, though I could feel the scarred edges of it and the way it slowed Gram's flow of magic.

"Gram," I choked out. "I'm so sorry." More tears. How had I failed her, of all people? Who never, ever once failed me.

Her hand slid over the covers slowly, a pale seeker finally finding my own. She squeezed gently and sighed. "You did what we raised you to do," Gram said. "You acted like a Hayle and took responsibility. I was the one who failed."

She'd finally cracked the rest of the way, clearly. "Gram—"

She closed her eyes, falling still for a moment and I did the same. Not the time to argue with her, I guess. Instead, I held her hand and flooded her with power and as much love as I could, still crying, more so as tears trickled from the corners of her eyes, too.

"Girl," Gram whispered. "I love you so much. You are truly the sister of my heart. Everything I've done, everything, has been for you." Her eyes opened again. "And I wouldn't change a thing."

I heard a soft sigh beside me, looked up to see Mom turning away, face twisted in grief.

I didn't need that kind of pressure right now. "I'm giving you back the family magic." Not only would it restore her—at least that was my hope—but I knew now it was the right thing to do. "I can't focus on what I have to do if I have the coven to worry about."

Gram's grip on my hand tightened, the fierce rejection in her eyes so powerful I actually felt better. "Just try it," she said. Coughed softly. "You have to lead this family. They need you." She paused, smiled a sweet smile, one I hadn't seen on her face since she regained her sanity. "We'll do it together." Her head turned, gaze going to Mom who spun around again. "All of us." Gram faced me, eyes shining with more tears. "I am so proud of you, girl," she said. "You are the daughter to me my poor Miriam never had the chance to be." Mom choked, fell still, hands clutched together, pressed to her chest. "It terrifies me, you know that? Sending you out there, to do the elements know what." Gram's cackle ended in a soft wheeze. "But I cheer you on every single time." She pulled on my hand and I leaned closer. "What an Enforcer you would have made," she breathed in my ear. Her free hand rose, fingers tracing over my cheek. "I always knew you were special. That you would be able to handle whatever this crazy life brought to you. And I was right."

Her hand dropped to the covers with a dull thud as her eyelids drooped. Sassafras's purr increased in volume as his power washed over her, calming her. She twitched, a little frown on her face as though she fought him, before sighing and falling into sleep.

I stayed there, frozen by her words, by her love, free hand pressed to my mouth to keep from sobbing out loud, still holding her hand.

So small and cold in mine.

Sassafras settled, amber eyes closing, nose to Gram's cheek as Mom circled the bed and helped me stand, guiding me from the room.

I leaned against the wall, entire being vibrating with the fear Gram wasn't going to be okay. That she said all those things because she knew she was dying. But Mom's hug came with a hearty dose of reassurance, as did Lula's kind smile.

"I promise," the young healer said, "Ethpeal isn't

going anywhere."

"For now" hung between us. But I'd take it.

"Syd," Mom said softly, "you have to understand. Your grandmother has been through so much, from her days as an Enforcer, her seventeen years when her mind was lost to us." Mom dabbed at her own tears. "Her body and mind are simply wearing out."

Too many battles. Too much grief and loss and endless suffering.

It had to get better from here for her. And I vowed, standing there outside her door, feeling the subtle support of Sassafras's power, I would make sure she had nothing but happiness from here on in.

If I had to kill anyone who came near her to do it.

CHAPTER FORTY

Liam's arms welcomed me as I appeared in the Sidhe cavern. I don't know if he expected me or if he was just that happy to see me. But the moment I showed up he rushed to me and hugged me tight.

Kissed me. And I kissed him back, the thrum of earth magic vibrating the ground beneath us.

When I finally pulled away, I giggled a little. "Forgot what that was like."

Wow, Syd. Way to prod a guy for being a pathetic Momma's boy.

Liam blushed, ducked his head. "We can see where it takes us," he said, hope in his face as his hands slid into my back pockets, tucking my hips against his. "If you want?"

Hmmm. "Where's your mother?" Come to think of

it, I hadn't seen her once since this whole thing started.

Liam's jaw tightened. "I sent her away."

Wow. He what?

"She was driving me nuts." He pulled free of me, turned to stare at the Gate. "I understood she felt guilty, that she was trying to protect me. But I couldn't take it anymore, Syd. So I made her leave."

"How?" Not that he wasn't persuasive if he wanted to be, but she was hard-core helicopter mom.

Liam turned to me, biting his lower lip, eyes full of guilt. "Magic," he said.

I choked on a laugh even though it really wasn't funny. "You did what?"

He tossed his hands in the air before running both of them through his strawberry blonde hair. "I know it was wrong." Liam clenched his fists at his sides, face compressing into a frown. "But she didn't give me a choice. She wanted me to seal the Gate, Syd. To give up my responsibility." He hesitated. "To give you up."

Way to find a backbone, Liam.

"I used my power," he said, starting to pace, clearly agitated by his choice. "She pushed me too far. Galleytrot was here." The big dog huffed a breath, tongue lolling out. He clearly found this whole situation amusing. "She yelled at me, talked about how dangerous the Gate was, how it killed Dad." Liam stopped moving, turned to me. "I snapped."

Venner, the Unseelie lordling we'd returned to the Sidhe realm killed Liam's father. But I still believed his mother had something to do with it.

Speaking of Venner, I hadn't seen him once during the crisis in the realm. I wondered if Odhran had done something nasty to him.

I could hope.

"I ordered her to go." Liam slumped. "With all of the power of the Gate behind me. And she did."

"Where?" I went to him, hugged him gently, rested my head on his chest while his arms rose and embraced me.

"I don't know," he whispered. "But I made sure she was safe. And happy. Told her to be. That was part of the order."

Of course it was. This was Liam, after all.

"When was this?" I looked up into his eyes.

"Two weeks ago." He stroked my hair back from my face.

"Why didn't you tell me?" Silly boy.

"Because," he said, clearly miserable, "you didn't want me anymore."

For a brief flash of time, Gram's face appeared in my mind. Her words. That he was weak, too weak for me.

But he'd kicked his own mother to the curb. For me. Well, for the Gate, too. But I was part of the package. That wasn't weak. Liam was stronger than anyone—

including me—gave him credit for. He just needed incentive to show his power.

I kissed him, let it linger. Felt his magic twine through mine. Remembered, in a tight knot of guilt, who I'd just kissed only a few hours ago.

Sighed internally as I stepped away from him.

"Well," I said. "Maybe we can try again."

Liam's beaming smile was all the answer I needed.

I stepped out of the veil into the yard not long after, leaving Liam to his research, not ready to rekindle things just yet, but feeling more hopeful. After all, I now had the power and permission to do what I needed to save the world, my one-time boyfriend proved he cared about me and his own responsibilities enough to act and Gram was going to be fine.

She was.

I just had to keep telling myself that.

I didn't get to walk into the house, not when the flare of power behind me turned me around. Quaid stepped out of the flash of blue light, chocolate eyes smiling at me.

And I ran right to his open arms.

Of course I did.

The moment he hugged me, face buried in my hair, he stiffened. Jerked back. Glared.

"I can smell him on you," Quaid said.

Freaking seriously? He was going to go into this now?

Quaid backed away, turned to leave.

How could I just let him go?

"Thank you," I said. "For being willing to throw everything away to save me."

He stopped, shoulders tight, body rigid. His head turned, profile nodding once. I stood there, willing him to just beat it. No, to turn around and get over here.

No. Wait.

Damn it all to the bowels of—

He spun, stomped to me, engulfed me in his arms and crushed me against him.

While my demon howled and pulled him closer.

Sparks raced through me, magic bursting in snaps of color, heat rising from the depths of my stomach, passion burning me, the pain too much and I wanted more, more, as much as I could get.

His lips lifted from mine and I whimpered, begging him not to stop. To never let me go.

Please, never.

"I'd die for you," he whispered over my mouth.

Released me. Backed away while the power tying us together fought for control.

And vanished in a flare of blue fire.

"Damn you," I whispered back. "Same here."

chapter forty one

I didn't make it two steps inside, still flushed from my encounter with Quaid, when I felt demon power surge in the basement and went running.

Found Meira waiting on the other side of the veil and crossed into her open arms.

She hugged me so tight I could barely breathe, forgetting until she pulled away to allow my demon form to take over.

Red skinned and black horned, I settled on her divan while she held my hand.

"Thanks for letting me know they didn't kill you or anything." She grinned, taking the sting out of her words.

"I was getting to it," I said. "Besides, you really thought they could?"

Meira's smile trembled and fell. "I didn't know," she

said.

We talked, about Gram, the Brotherhood. My new freedom. Meira's fierce, "Awesome!" mirrored my own.

"I'm worried about Demonicon now," I said. "The Brotherhood has failed with the Sidhe and at least one major vampire clan. They will probably be coming for you next." I paused, heart tightening all over again. "If they aren't here already. You know how insidious they can be. How subtly their invasion begins."

Meira just patted my hand with a grim smile on her face.

"Let them," she said, tossing back her long, black curls. "I'm ready."

Not "we". Made me wonder. "How's Dad?"

Meira's pause before answering told me volumes. "He's fine," she said. "Still settling in as Ruler."

I opened my mouth to comment only to have Meira shake her head with a look of guilt.

"I shouldn't say that," she said. "He's a wonderful Ruler. He's just…"

"Dad," I said. "Kind and loving and generous."

Meira's eyes told me I was right.

Which meant our demon family walked all over him.

"And Henemordonin?" At least he had a soul of steel.

"Grandfather is doing his best," Meira said. "But Dad has his own ideas."

Happiness and sparkly perkiness for all demons.

That would work.

"You know," I said, "you were the right choice. I'd have made a terrible Ruler. But you, you're going to kick ass someday."

She laughed. "I don't know if that's a compliment or not." Her nose wrinkled before she squeezed my hand. "It is," she said. "And I hope you're right."

I hugged her. "I really have to get back. But please, let's not have this much time go between us from now on." I pulled away. "Regular contact."

"Promise." She stood and I joined her. "But you can't go yet. Someone wants to talk to you."

I winced, thinking who that someone might be. Followed her to the sitting room adjacent to her bedchamber. Found Rameranselot waiting for me.

Meira kissed me, winked and left us alone.

Bratski.

Ram's smirk triggered my temper, but also made me laugh. I crossed to him, hugged him. Felt my demon's passions stir again.

Felt like a total trollop. Three guys, Syd? Really? Not counting Sage, my martial arts teacher. Oh, and Sebastian.

Damn it. I had to free Sebastian.

But I had less than a year, didn't I? Maybe the more the merrier, if it meant I made the best choice out of the options I had.

Since the right choice wasn't open to me.

Ram's lips found mine, with a hunger I wasn't expecting. I kissed him back, opening to him as I'd never done before, letting my demon have full reign. But she pulled away after a moment, as lovely and delicious as he was.

Comparing him to Quaid wasn't conducive to encouraging a relationship.

"Were you serious?" His amber eyes didn't show me anything but his natural sarcastic humor. He was a master at hiding how he felt.

I didn't say anything, trying to decide. Was I? I asked him if he'd consider an effigy, knowing full well he'd know what I meant. What I offered.

Before I could decide, Ram laughed and hugged me, broad chest hard under my hands.

"I'm not who you need," he said. "Who is he?"

Sigh.

"Someone I can never have," I said. Felt the sting of tears again.

Stupid tears. Piss off already.

Ram let me go, smirk gone. Kissed my forehead.

"I knew better than to open my heart to you," he said. "From the moment we met, I understood you'd never be mine. But it didn't work out the way I planned." He grinned, a boyish expression that made me smile. "Still. I guess you'll just have to keep looking, princess."

I stepped back from him, reaching for the veil. Felt

my demon grandmother's spirit answer. Met Ram's eyes before I stepped through the gap. "Watch over her," I said. "Keep my sister safe."

He bowed, one hand pressed to his chest, absolutely serious. "I will give my life for hers," he said. "I swear it."

The echo of that was so familiar I stumbled my way through the veil.

Landed in the basement.

Realized only then, in the dark silence, I was alone.

Totally. Utterly. No, my egos were still with me. But one very important person wasn't.

Charlotte.

My head snapped up, terror punching me in the stomach.

"Charlotte?" When had I seen her last? I dove for the stairs, took them two at a time, calling her name. I couldn't remember when I saw her. No, wait. I could.

Lying face down over the threshold of the back door. Blood pooling from her mouth and nose—

No. No, she couldn't be dead, they would have told me. And she'd only just chose to come back from the brink to be with me.

"Charlotte!"

I pounded up the stairs, hearing Shenka call for me from the living room, raced into Charlotte's room, my old room, without knocking. Guilt gnawed at my soul. How had I forgotten her?

How?

I froze at the sight of the perfectly made bed, the open closet door.

Empty.

Her things missing, not even the scent of her left behind.

My eyes fell to the quilt, to a piece of paper. Numb, lost, I picked it up. Unfolded it.

Я тебе кохаю. Carefully written in Charlotte's tight, efficient handwriting.

I sank to the bed, chest tightening around grief as Shenka burst into the room, concern on her face.

"Syd," she looked around, clearly as confused by the emptiness as I was. "Where's Charlotte?"

I bent over the note, the letters smearing from my tears, no idea what the words meant, but cherishing them anyway.

Because they were all I had left of her.

Charlotte   was   gone.

Chapter Forty Two

Fairy tale endings are highly overrated.

At least, that's what I kept telling myself so I wouldn't feel so crappy about my life.

Demetrius returned, no sign of Alison. And the Brotherhood seemed to have gone to ground. I really hoped I did some major damage to Belaisle, both with the freeing of the Sidhe and by taking back the power of the Council. And Mom. He had to have been pouring a ton of energy into my mother.

Sucked to be him.

Not to mention all the magic Ameline stole. I had no doubt Belaisle would simply drain some of his own people to replace it, but it had to rankle.

Rankling was good.

Mind you, I wished the Brotherhood were out in the

open instead of scurrying around like cockroaches looking for scraps at 3AM.

Gross.

At least with the Council's approval to act, I could start hunting them down and squashing them. That would be awesome.

I just had to find them first.

I had the sheet of paper Charlotte left me translated by a sweet older Russian woman who ran the local coffee shop. She squinted at it a moment before beaming me a smile and a wink. Told me it said "I love you" in Ukrainian.

I figured it was something like that.

But even though I tried to find her in those first hours and days, I finally gave up searching for my bodywere. Charlotte left on purpose, chose to go. And I now could only guess the bond keeping her with me had broken, probably when she almost died. Why I hadn't noticed...? Yeah, more guilt.

Dummyhead.

It wasn't my enemies I had to worry about. Sooner or later my own guilt would kill me.

I let her go, as hard as it was, knowing if she decided to come back, she would. That was Charlotte. But I still wished I could have said goodbye and wondered almost daily if she was okay.

I had to release my need to chase down Ameline, too.

That one hurt just as much, only in a different way. Like someone ground a dull knife in my guts kind of way rather than shattering my heart into tiny fragments.

Fun times.

Ameline was necessary. Had to develop her power. Fine. Okay then. She could just do that and hurry the hell up about it so we could track down the Brotherhood and smoosh them.

And then, I would kill her. Happily. With a big smile on my face.

Couldn't wait.

Made it so much worse knowing I needed her.

Gram was recovering somewhat, though her happy-go-crazy attitude had dimmed. I often found her sitting alone in the kitchen, just staring into space. Gone were her fuzzy socks, her cackling laugh. She cried a lot, when she'd let me catch her at it, and I often found Sassafras sneaking in to her room to sleep with her.

She needed him way more than I did, so I was cool with that. Any comfort he could bring her was a good thing.

When Varity visited the first time, she hugged me. Apologized all over again. I felt about three inches tall knowing I'd lied to her and gotten away with it. Mind you, I could have told her the truth, knowing there was nothing she could do about it, but seeing her made Gram happy so I swallowed my regret and welcomed the old

Enforcer leader whenever she came to call.

Uncle Frank and Sunny were in close contact, which was a nice change. Sunny happily reported her entire blood clan, from the top down, was clear of the taint. She was concerned still about the Sthol's, though, through the small interactions the other queen allowed her. Mom mentioned she heard a mutter of complaint from Pannera about me showing up at her castle, but she happily informed me since it was vampire business, it had nothing to do with her, did it?

Finally. The rules worked our way for once.

Sebastian crossed my mind many times over the next few weeks, but when I brought him up to Mom, she finally had to put her foot down. Yes, I had permission to act. In our territory. And while technically Celeste and her blood clan—Sebastian's blood clan—chose to live in North America, they were under the rule of the Sthol clan in Austria.

And thus, in Margaret Applegate's purview.

Which meant I had to stay out of it. We argued about it, but it was normal arguing. Mom and Syd arguing. Almost fun, if it wasn't for the seriousness of the subject matter, just like old times. And, in the end, though it broke my heart to leave him there, I knew Sebastian had been through and survived worse. Didn't stop me from swearing to myself I'd find a way to help him, no matter what it took.

No more forgetting about family and friends because I fell into a lull coma.

No more.

Mom spent a lot of time in Wilding Springs, the pair of us, and Gram included when she showed interest, talking about our plans. What to do next. How to protect the covens. Mom mentioned a world conclave, hosting it here. As a way to check in on the other High Councils, to see how far the Brotherhood's influence had spread. I shuddered at the thought of managing those logistics and told her it was a great idea.

If I couldn't go to their territories to do my job, we'd bring them to mine.

The coolest part of all of the time we spent together? I felt like I finally had my mother back. Stronger and more powerful than ever.

Meira's reports came frequently. All quiet on the Demonicon front. She even joined us for dinner from time to time. All we were missing was Dad and we'd be one big happy family again.

Sigh.

Trill and her brothers were gone by the time I was released, but I heard from her shortly after my meltdown over Charlotte. She hadn't worried about me even for a second, knew I'd be fine. Was in pursuit of a dark maji who might be able to give her information on the Brotherhood. I let her go with the promise she'd stay in touch.

Look at me, going all protective and stuff.

Quaid kept his distance and I didn't blame him. He had to be as screwed up about his feelings for me as I was. And Liam's quiet patience made me wish I could just cut Quaid off and move on already.

Especially when I heard from Meira, whispering to me one night with tears in her eyes, Dad had finally narrowed his bride list down to three candidates. That he wanted me to meet them.

Oh *hell* no. How many kinds of wrong was that? Even my demon protested. Like some slimy high-Plane step mother was someone I was interested in coming face-to-face with, playing nicey-nice just to satisfy our demon family.

Gag. Besides, I was just too loyal to Mom.

But in the back of my mind, as the rest of my stress churned and I thought about Dad's pending marriage, my own threatened in the distance.

Wedding bells?

More like the deep tolling of my impending doom.

Married by twenty-one, huh?

I was so screwed.

Like what you read? Find out more at
pattilarsen.com

Here's a look at the first chapter of
Book Seventeen of the Hayle Coven Novels

shifting Loyalties

CHAPTER ONE

I choked on a French fry as Tippy's punch line made me blush and laugh at the same time. As outrageous as ever, the red-haired Hensley witch winked at me, substantial rack pushing the giant rude hand gesture on her chest into everyone's face. She'd forgiven me for choosing Shenka as my second almost as fast as she'd gotten over the fact Liam and I were an item. Sort of an item. I glanced sideways at him, found him blushing just as brightly as I knew I was and laughed privately.

He'd never survive Tippy even if hc was into her.

Hell, I still worried if he'd survive me.

Not going there, not right now. I'd had a great, quiet fall, a lovely Christmas holiday at home with Meira making an appearance despite her permanent relocation to Demonicon. Mom was herself again, young, beautiful, enthusiastic. And though still stressed from her job, she was no longer under the control of the Brotherhood, her natural ability to balance work and home almost eerie.

No complaining. I was just happy to have my mother back.

It was almost hard to come back to Harvard for my last semester, to leave the happiness of my house, feeling almost as though nothing changed. Though so much had. Gram was the biggest indicator, quiet and withdrawn, crabby most of the time, she locked herself in her bedroom more often than not. Broke my heart, knowing how much she suffered from the loss of her magic.

To Ameline of all people. I still owed that bitch for hurting my grandmother. Would kill her for it one day. Just as soon as my maji guide, Iepa, told me I didn't need the evil witch anymore.

Talk about a mood downer. I set aside my fork, shoulders slumping despite the giggling going on around me. I wasn't really listening anymore. Besides, I was tired, worn out. I'd let so many people down in the past, forgetting their problems, allowing too much to slide. No more. Which meant almost constant contact with a large group of loved ones. Regular visits to Austria to see Sunny and Uncle Frank, to the Sidhe realm to check in on the now single court of the Fey. Almost daily chats with my sister, partly out of the need to keep her safe and partly because I just missed her.

And the coven. Always the coven. Shenka was great, I

had to admit. I met her eyes as she rolled hers at me while Tippy brayed her excessive laugh. I loved my second, knew I'd made the perfect choice sneaking her out from under her sister, Tallah. She insisted on joining me for every visit she could attend, even trying to cross to Demonicon with me, though we both knew it wouldn't work out. The only one who'd been able to join me was Charlotte, my bodywere, which led me to believe she had demon ancestry somewhere in her makeup.

Thinking of Charlotte just made things worse. I still thought of her as "mine" even though she left me months ago, the bond between us broken. She came back from the dead for me, when I think she might have chosen to pass over in another circumstance. But then she'd left, with only a note telling me she loved me in Ukrainian. I hadn't heard from her in all that time. Yes, I was focused on keeping an eye on those I cared about to be sure they were okay, but in Charlotte's case, she'd made it pretty clear she didn't want contact.

And no matter how much I hated the fact she was out there on her own, I had to honor that.

Mostly.

Shenka set aside her napkin, pushing her tray away. The dark, early evening sky pressed against the stained glass behind her, window rimmed in frost of deep January.

"I'm off for home." Right, I'd forgotten. It was Friday

already, the normal crowd of students in the cafeteria thinned with the onset of the weekend. We'd both acquired the habit of returning to Wilding Springs when we didn't have class. More family time. And while I looked forward to it for the most part, the idea of staying at school and getting some well-earned sleep seemed like a good idea.

No rest for the wicked.

Liam's hand fell on my arm as the small posse of girls rose. Nicci Mortimer, freckles pushing together as she wrinkled her nose and winked at me, turned, one arm sliding through Tippy's to guide her away while Donalda Pierce blew us both a kiss, gray eyes sparkling, before joining them, tall, thin body towering over the smaller pair. Shenka paused, a sweet smile on her face, turning her back to give us a moment.

Which made me nervous they knew something I didn't.

"I was thinking," Liam said in his deep voice, hazel eyes sparking with points of green as his cheeks pinked, tongue running nervously over his lips.

"That's got to hurt." I laughed and squeezed his hand as he snorted. "Go on."

Liam relaxed, my irreverence seeming to put him at ease for whatever he was after. "You've been working so hard these past few months," at least someone noticed, "I thought maybe you could let Shenka go home this weekend." He paused. Swallowed. "Alone." Paused again while my chest tightened. "So you could stay with me."

Oh. Boy.

I'd been waffling over him, over what to do about us. Didn't help I only had a few months left before I was supposed to get married. Still gave me shivers and made me want to pack up and run for the hills thinking about it. His sweet offer was obviously some kind of bid to spend some time and see if we could reconnect.

Shenka glanced over her shoulder, eyebrows raised. I knew then she was in full cahoots with him, but not in the way he thought. She waited, patient and 100% on my side, ready to support me no matter what I chose to do. As I looked back to Liam, the anxiety in his face, the way he bent his body toward mine, I thought of Gram.

She'd told me once he was too weak for me. That he was a terrible choice. And that held me back, too.

But there was only one way to find out if she was right. Which meant exploring this relationship at last. Images of other faces passed before me. Of Ram, my demon friend who I knew now I'd never choose to be my mate. But there were more, at least two more. One I pined for almost every day despite my best intentions. And the other I'd been trying desperately to free since August.

My appeals to Applegate on Sebastian's behalf fell on deaf ears, every attempt Mom and I made to release the imprisoned former blood clan leader ignored. I knew I could simply storm into the vampire mansion and take out their current leader, Celeste Oberman. Wanted to, so very much. Would enjoy watching her wither and burn in the sun after all the horrible things she'd done to my family when she was a Hayle witch. But Mom insisted we use diplomacy despite both of us knowing Sebastian was suffering at Celeste's hand.

He was my friend, but more than that. He'd expressed his interest at Sunny and Uncle Frank's wedding and thanks to my immortality, choosing him was a distinct possibility. But I couldn't marry a vampire who I couldn't reach.

That left one.

I just couldn't go there. To those chocolate eyes, that smirk. Delicious magic threading through mine. Creak of leather, the way his long, wavy hair hung, begging to be touched.

All of him. Begging.

Growl.

Oh snap. I shook myself a little as Liam touched my cheek with his fingertips just as Shenka's mind poked mine.

You suck at this, she sent with laughter in her mental voice. *Give the poor boy a break would you?* She turned to face me, already gathering her things. *I'll see you later.*

She left me there, a wave for Liam, as I pulled myself

out of comparing the handsome, sweet guy in front of me to the other options I had for marriage like he was an under ripe watermelon.

What the hell was wrong with me?

"Sorry," I said, clasping his hands in mine. "Space cadet moment."

He bobbed a nod, started to pull away, his disappointment clear on his face.

"I understand," he said. "You have so much on your plate. Family and responsibility come first for both of us. It was stupid for me to ask."

I tugged him back, forcing myself to relax. A weekend off with Liam? I could handle that.

"I'd love to," I said.

And really meant it. Imagine that.

About the Author

Everything you need to know about me is in this one statement: I've wanted to be a writer since I was a little girl, and now I'm doing it. How cool is that, being able to follow your dream and make it reality? I've tried everything from university to college, graduating the second with a journalism diploma (I sucked at telling real stories), am part of an all-girl improv troupe (if you've never tried it, I highly recommend making things up as you go along as often as possible). I've even been in a Celtic girl band (some of our stuff is on YouTube!) and was an independent film maker. My life has been one creative thing after another—all leading me here, to writing books for a living.

Now with multiple series in happy publication, I live on beautiful and magical Prince Edward Island (I know you've heard of Anne of Green Gables) with my very patient husband and multitude of pets.

I love-love-love hearing from you! You can reach me (and I promise I'll message back) at patti@pattilarsen.com. And if you're eager for your next dose of Patti Larsen books (usually about one release a month) come join my mailing list! All the best up and coming, giveaways, contests and, of course, my observations on the world (aren't you just dying to know what I think about everything?) all in one place: http://smarturl.it/PattiLarsenEmail.

Last—but not least!—I hope you enjoyed what you read! Your happiness is my happiness. And I'd love to hear just what you thought. A review where you found this book would mean the world to me—reviews feed writers more than you will ever know. So, loved it (or not so much), **your honest review would make my day**. Thank you!